"What happened to me?" Brooke whispered brokenly, her breath rasping. "Have I been ill?"

"You were in an accident." The doctor paused there, exchanging a glance with the staff surrounding the bed.

"What's my name?" she asked shakily.

"Your name is Brooke...Brooke Tassini."

The name meant absolutely nothing to her, didn't even sound slightly familiar.

"Your husband will be here very soon."

Brooke's eyes widened to their fullest extent in shock. "I have a husband?"

For some reason, the nurses smiled. "Oh, yes, you have a husband."

"A very handsome husband," one of the women added.

Brooke stared down at her bare wedding finger. She was married. Oh, my goodness, she was married.

D0040602

Passion in Paradise

Exotic escapes...and red-hot romances!

Step into a jet-set world where first class is the *only* way to travel. From Monte Carlo to Tuscany, you'll find a billionaire at every turn! But no billionaire is complete without the perfect romance. Especially when that passion is found in the most incredible destinations...

Find out what happens in:

The Innocent's Forgotten Wedding by Lynne Graham

The Italian's Pregnant Cinderella by Caitlin Crews

Kidnapped for His Royal Heir by Maya Blake

His Greek Wedding Night Debt by Michelle Smart

The Spaniard's Surprise Love-Child by Kim Lawrence

My Shocking Monte Carlo Confession by Heidi Rice

A Bride Fit for a Prince? by Susan Stephens

A Scandal Made in London by Lucy King

Available this month!

Lynne Graham

—

THE INNOCENT'S
FORGOTTEN WEDDING

HARLEQUIN

PRESENTS

If you purchased this book without a cover you should be aware that this book is stolen property. It was reported as "unsold and destroyed" to the publisher, and neither the author nor the publisher has received any payment for this "stripped book."

Recycling programs for this product may not exist in your area.

ISBN-13: 978-1-335-89356-7

The Innocent's Forgotten Wedding

Copyright © 2020 by Lynne Graham

All rights reserved. No part of this book may be used or reproduced in any manner whatsoever without written permission except in the case of brief quotations embodied in critical articles and reviews.

This is a work of fiction. Names, characters, places and incidents are either the product of the author's imagination or are used fictitiously. Any resemblance to actual persons, living or dead, businesses, companies, events or locales is entirely coincidental.

This edition published by arrangement with Harlequin Books S.A.

For questions and comments about the quality of this book, please contact us at CustomerService@Harlequin.com.

Harlequin Enterprises ULC
22 Adelaide St. West, 40th Floor
Toronto, Ontario M5H 4E3, Canada
www.Harlequin.com

Printed in U.S.A.

Lynne Graham was born in Northern Ireland and has been a keen romance reader since her teens. She is very happily married to an understanding husband who has learned to cook since she started to write! Her five children keep her on her toes. She has a very large dog who knocks everything over, a very small terrier who barks a lot and two cats. When time allows, Lynne is a keen gardener.

Books by Lynne Graham

Harlequin Presents

The Greek's Blackmailed Mistress
The Italian's Inherited Mistress
Indian Prince's Hidden Son

Conveniently Wed!

The Greek's Surprise Christmas Bride

One Night With Consequences

His Cinderella's One-Night Heir

Billionaires at the Altar

The Greek Claims His Shock Heir
The Italian Demands His Heirs
The Sheikh Crowns His Virgin

Vows for Billionaires

The Secret Valtinos Baby
Castiglione's Pregnant Princess
Da Rocha's Convenient Heir

Visit the Author Profile page
at Harlequin.com for more titles.

CHAPTER ONE

MILLY'S HEARTBEAT SPEEDED UP with excitement when she saw Brooke's name flash across the screen of her cheap mobile because it had been a while since she had heard from her famous and glamorous half-sister.

When Brooke phoned, however, it meant that Brooke *needed* her and that truth more than made up for Brooke's often cold and seemingly critical attitude towards her. Milly loved being needed and, in any case, deep down inside, Milly was convinced that her sister *cared* about her even though she might be too proud to admit it.

After all, why else would Brooke confide in her about so many private things if she did not, at heart, see Milly as a trustworthy friend and sister? Furthermore, aside of each other, neither one of them had a single living relative. Nor was it surprising that Brooke would need her services again when her life was in such turmoil, thanks to that dreadful possessive tyrant of a man she had mistakenly married. What sort of a man would try and come between Brooke and her career? What sort of man would divorce a wife as beautiful and talented as Brooke simply over ugly rumours that she had had an affair?

'He won't listen to a word I say!' Brooke had wept when she'd confided in Milly. 'He set me up because he wants rid of me. I'm convinced he *paid* that creep to lure me into a hotel room and lie about having sex with me!'

'Brooke?' Milly exclaimed warmly as she answered her phone.

'I need you to pretend to be me for a few days.'

'A few...*days*?' Milly stressed in dismay, for that request went far beyond anything her sister had asked of her before. 'Are you sure I'll be able to manage that? I'm OK until people speak to me and expect me to be you!'

'You'll be holed up in a fancy hotel in the heart of London,' Brooke told her drily. 'You won't be required to talk to anyone but room service. You won't need to leave the room at all.'

Milly frowned. 'For how long?' she pressed anxiously.

'Five or six days. That's all,' Brooke informed her briskly.

'I *can't*, Brooke,' Milly protested apologetically. 'I've got a job and I don't want to lose it.'

'You're a waitress, Milly, not a brain surgeon,' her half-sister reminded her tartly. 'You can pick up casual work anywhere at this time of year. And if it's a matter of me paying your rent *again* for you, I'll do it!'

Milly flushed and subsided again because it was true, she could find another job relatively easily, and if Brooke made up her loss of wages to cover the rent on her bedsit as well, she had no grounds for complaint either. When it occurred to her that she had ended up sleeping on a friend's sofa the last time she'd needed help to cover her rent, she suppressed the memory. Brooke had forgotten to give her the money she had promised but Milly felt that that oversight was her own fault because she had been too embarrassed to remind Brooke. She couldn't help but shrink from highlighting the financial differences between her and her sister, and wasn't one bit surprised that Brooke had always refused to be seen in public with her or invite her into her more exciting world even briefly, except in Milly's guise as a lookalike. What else could she expect? Milly asked herself ruefully. In truth, she was lucky to have *any* kind of relationship with her sibling at all…

Brooke had first sought out Milly when she was eighteen and fresh out of a council home for foster kids. Milly had already known that she was illegitimate, but she had been shocked by what her newly discovered half-sister had to tell her—well, shocked and initially repulsed by Brooke's view of the circumstances of her birth. But then, slowly, she had come to understand Brooke's feelings of betrayal and had forgiven her sister for her offensive wording.

'Your mother was the slut who almost broke up my parents' happy marriage!' Brooke had told her sharply.

To be fair to Brooke, Milly's mother *had* been the other woman who slept with a married man, inflicting considerable suffering on that man's innocent wife and child. Brooke and Milly's father, William Jackson, a wealthy wine importer, had had a long-running affair with a model called Natalia Taylor and had threatened to leave his wife over her.

Sadly, a heart attack had taken William's life when Brooke was fifteen and Milly was nine. Natalia had died in a bus crash only a couple of years later and Milly had ended up in council care, where she had remained until she reached eighteen. At first meeting, both young women had been taken aback by the likeness between them, for they had both inherited their father's white-blonde curly hair and dark blue eyes. Milly, however, had had a large bump in her nose and somehow the features that made Brooke a stunning beauty had blurred in Milly's case, putting her into the pretty rather than beautiful category.

It had been Brooke's idea that she could use Milly as a stand-in either to avoid an event she considered boring or, more frequently, to mislead the paparazzi that dogged her footsteps and who occasionally followed her places where she didn't want to be seen or photographed her with individuals whom she didn't wish to be seen with. Brooke was obsessed with airbrushing and controlling the public image she wanted to show the world.

In the same way she had pointed out that Milly couldn't help her unless she was prepared to go that extra mile and have her nose 'done' so that it mirrored Brooke's far more elegant nose. At first, Milly had said a very firm no to that idea, not because she was fond of her less than perfect nose but just because it was hers and she was accustomed to her own flaws.

Brooke had had a huge row with her over her refusal and Milly had been devastated when her half-sister had cut off all contact with her. When Brooke had called her again six weeks later, Milly had been so grateful to hear from her that she had agreed to the surgical procedure and before she could change her mind she had been whisked into a private clinic and her nose had been skilfully enhanced to resemble Brooke's. Once that had been achieved, expert make-up had completed her transformation.

The first time Milly had pretended to be

Brooke to enable her sister to evade a boring charity event, she had been terrified, even dressed in her sister's clothes and made up to look like her, but nobody had suspected a thing and, for the first time in her life, Milly had felt like an achiever. Brooke's gratitude had made her feel wonderfully warm inside and the second time, when Milly had had to simply step out of a limousine and walk into a shop while Brooke was many miles away, she had felt even better. She had discovered that it was fun to dress up in expensive clothes and pretend to be someone she was not and there had been very little fun in Milly's life before Brooke entered it.

And with Brooke in her current predicament, struggling to deal with her broken marriage, Milly knew that she should definitely go that extra mile for her sister. 'Where will you be while I sit in this hotel?' she asked curiously.

'Having a very discreet little holiday, so I'll need your passport,' Brooke advanced. 'I daren't travel on my own.'

And Milly frowned at that reference to her passport but could only smile at the mention of a holiday. A holiday was exactly what her poor sister needed at this stressful time in her life and if Milly room-sitting in some fancy hotel was all that was required, it would be utterly selfish of her to refuse to help. 'OK. I'll do it.'

'You can only bring one small bag with you. I've packed a case for you, and you can change into my clothes in the car,' Brooke informed her. 'I'll do your make-up in the car too. I'm better at it than you are.'

After Brooke had arranged to pick her up, Milly straightened her hair and threw her passport, fresh underwear, a couple of books and a range of craft items into a bag before heading out. It was a filthy wet day and she didn't step out onto the pavement until she had her umbrella up to protect her hair for Brooke's hair was always a perfect blonde fall without even a hint of curl.

First, however, Milly took ten minutes to walk down the street and quit her waitressing job in a local café, mentioning a family emergency. She hated letting people down, but Brooke had been right, she would probably find another job quite quickly, she reasoned, guilty at having let an employer she liked down at short notice. But, my goodness, Brooke *did* deserve a holiday after everything she had recently been through and if she could help her sibling achieve that, then she could be proud of herself because family needs came first, family should *always* come first, she thought ruefully, regretting that neither of her parents had lived by that truth.

Brooke looked amazing when Milly glimpsed her inside the limo, all groomed and flawless in a black jacket, a tomato-red sheath dress and very high-heeled stilettos. It was likely, though, to be a struggle for her sibling to get out of that dress in the back of the limo, no matter how spacious it was, Milly ruminated.

'Quick, get in!' Brooke snapped at her. 'We can't be seen together!'

'What about the driver?' Milly asked in bemusement as the passenger door closed to seal the two women into privacy.

'I pay him well to keep quiet!' Brooke fielded, snapping shut the privacy screen between the front and the rear seats. 'Now help me out of this dress... Oh, yes, don't forget that I need your passport too.'

'It has to be against the law for you to

travel on my passport,' Milly muttered uncomfortably. 'Do you *have* to borrow it?'

Brooke settled furious dark blue eyes on her. 'I don't have a choice. I'll be traced if I travel under my own name. With your name, I'm nobody, and nobody is the slightest bit interested in me or where I go.'

Reluctantly accepting that reality, Milly handed over her passport and proceeded to help her sibling out of her tight dress.

'Good grief, I don't see you for a couple of months and you let yourself turn into the ugly sister. Your nails are awful!' Brooke complained, snatching at one of Milly's hands to frown down at the sight of nails that were an unpainted and modest length. 'I'm always perfectly groomed. When you're checking in, keep them hidden and get a manicurist to come to the room and fix them before you check out again!' she instructed impatiently.

'I'm sorry,' Milly muttered, choosing not to point out that she couldn't afford to have her nails done professionally. Brooke regarded expensive treatments in the beauty field as essential maintenance and never

ever considered the cost of them. 'When do you think you'll be back?'

'Hell…you're putting on weight again too, aren't you?' Brooke said in frustration as she urged Milly to breathe in to enable her to get the zip up on the fitted dress.

Milly had been born curvier and almost an inch shorter than Brooke and she didn't respond. She knew she wasn't overweight but since meeting Brooke, who was thinner, she had deliberately dropped almost a stone so that she could fit better into her sister's clothes. Unfortunately, that had meant avoiding all her favourite comfort foods and reining in her love of chocolate. Beside her, Brooke kicked off her shoes and began to dress in jeans and a long concealing top, bundling her hair up under a peaked cap. Digging into her bag she produced moist wipes and began to wipe off her make-up.

'It's like being a spy,' Milly remarked with helpless amusement.

'Don't be so childish, Milly!' Brooke snapped impatiently. 'Have you any idea how much is riding on this holiday I'm having? This is too important to joke about. I'm meeting someone while I'm away who may put my name forward for a film part.'

'Well, it's exciting for me,' Milly confided with a little wrinkle of her nose and a look of guilty apology. 'Sorry. I expect it'll be pretty boring stuck in that hotel room though, so this is the fun part.'

'You'll need my rings…for goodness' sake, don't lose them! I may need to sell them somewhere down the road,' Brooke admitted stiffly, threading her wedding and engagement rings off her long manicured finger and passing them over. 'That *bastard*, Lorenzo! He could have slung me a few million for the sake of it, but he stuck to the letter of the pre-nup. I'm not getting a penny I'm not due. Still, he'll just be a bad memory a few years down the road. My next husband will be a fashion icon or an actor, *not* a banker!'

Disappointed by her sister's bad mood, Milly donned the rings and slid her feet into the shoes while Brooke passed her bag and jacket over. 'Do you think that when you come back we could spend an evening together?' she asked hesitantly.

'Why would I want to do that?' Brooke demanded.

'It's been ages since we spent any real time together,' Milly pointed out quietly. 'I would really enjoy that and maybe talking over things would make you feel better.'

'I'm feeling fine.' Brooke snapped open the privacy screens and lifted her make-up kit before pausing to communicate with the driver and telling him to speed up because she didn't want to check in late for her flight. 'When I first went looking for you, I was curious about you. But I'm not curious any more. I've been very good to you too, sprucing you up, fixing your face. What more can you expect from me? It's not as though we could ever be friends, not with your mother having slept with my father while he was still married to *my* mother. Do you realise that my poor mother tried to *kill* herself over their affair?'

Milly paled at that new revelation and dropped her head. 'I am so sorry, Brooke, but I've been hoping that in time…well, that we could get over that history because we're still sisters.'

Brooke pushed up Milly's chin to outline

her mouth with lip liner. 'Smile…yes, that's the ticket. There is no getting over the fact that your mother shagged my father and I don't do friends. Friends let you down and talk behind your back.'

'I wouldn't *ever*!' Milly protested.

'Well, you haven't so far,' Brooke conceded grudgingly. 'And you've been very useful to me, I'll agree. But we have nothing in common, Milly. You're poor and uneducated and you wouldn't even be able to talk properly if I hadn't sent you to elocution classes. You knit and you go to libraries. What would we talk about? I'd be bored stiff with you in five minutes.'

Milly paled and stiffened and called herself all kinds of a fool for running blindly into such abuse. She had closed her eyes too long to Brooke's essential coldness towards her, hoping that Brooke would eventually accept her as her sister and leave the sins of their mutual parents behind her in the past where they belonged. But for the first time, she was recognising that Brooke was as angry and resentful now about their father's affair as she had been when she'd first met her. Brooke tucked away her make-up kit and told the driver yet again to speed up, the instruction sharp and irritable in tone.

The rain had got so heavy that it was streaming down the windows and visibility was poor. It was a horrible day weather-wise, Milly conceded wryly, suppressing her hurt at being labelled boring. It was true that she and her sister had little in common apart from their paternity and their physical likeness to one another. Evidently, however, Brooke didn't feel an atom of a deeper connection to her because of their blood bond. When Brooke had confided in her about her problems, had it meant anything to her at all? Possibly, Brooke had grasped that Milly was trustworthy in that line and unlikely to reveal all to some murky tabloid newspaper. Or maybe Milly had just been there at the right moment when Brooke had needed to unburden herself.

'This will be the last time I stand in for you, Brooke,' Milly said quietly but firmly. 'If I'm honest, I kind of wish I'd never started it.'

'Oh, for heaven's sake, why do you have to start getting difficult right now?' Brooke demanded wrathfully.

'I'm not being difficult and I'm not about to let you down,' Milly responded tautly. 'But once this is over, I won't be acting as your stand-in again.'

Brooke flashed one of her charming smiles and stretched out her hand to squeeze Milly's. 'I'm sorry if I've been short with you but this has been such a frantic rush and I'm living on my nerves. We're almost at your hotel. Make sure you don't get into any conversations with staff. I never chat to menial people. Stay in your room and eat there too and don't eat any rubbish. I am known for my healthy eating regime and I have an exercise video in the pipeline. You can't be seen after you've checked in. People will understand. They know my marriage is over and I wouldn't look human if I wasn't seen to be grieving and in need of some private downtime…'

Milly was not fooled by that fake smile or the apology. She could see that she was only receiving it because Brooke was scared she would pull out on her at the last minute and it saddened her to see that lack of real feeling in the sister she had come to care deeply for.

Their driver was travelling fast when he suddenly jammed on the brakes to a jolting halt to make a turn. Milly peered out at the traffic. There was a large truck coming through red stop lights towards them and she gasped in fear.

Beside her Brooke was shouting at the driver and as Milly braced herself and offered up a silent prayer she tried to reach out for Brooke's hand, but her sister was screaming and she couldn't reach her. There was a terrible crunch on impact that jarred every bone in her body and then she blacked out in response to the wave of unimaginable pain that engulfed every part of her. Brooke... *Brooke*, she wanted to shriek in horror, because her sister had released her seat belt while she was changing...

Lorenzo Tassini, the most exceptional private banker of his generation and a renowned genius in the field of finance, was in an unusually good mood that morning because his soon-to-be ex-wife had finally signed the divorce papers earlier that day.

It was done. Within a few weeks, Lorenzo would be free, *finally* free, from a wife who'd lied, cheated, slept around and created endless embarrassing headlines in the newspapers. Brooke hoped to build an acting career on the back of her notoriety. Lorenzo might despise her, but he blamed himself more for his poor judgement in marrying her than he blamed her for letting him down. In retrospect, he could barely comprehend the madness that had taken hold of him when he had first met Brooke Jackson, a woman totally outside his wide and varied experience of the opposite sex. Lust had proved to be his downfall, he reflected grimly.

Brooke's white-blonde beauty had mesmerised him but the two years he had been with her had been filled with rage, regret and bitterness, for the honeymoon period in their marriage had been of very short duration. The ink had barely been dry on their marriage licence before he'd realised that his dream of having a wife who would give him a happy home life was unlikely to come true with a woman who had absolutely no interest in making a home or in having a child or indeed spending time with him any place other than a noisy nightclub.

But then what did *he* know about having a happy home life? Or even about having a family? Indeed, Lorenzo would've been the first to admit his ignorance in those fields. He, after all, had been raised in a regimented Italian palazzo by a father who cared more about his academic triumphs than his happiness or comfort. Strict nannies and home tutors had raised him to follow in the footsteps of his forebears and put profit first, and his dream of leading a more normal life in a comfortable home had died on the back of Brooke's first betrayal. All that foolish nonsense was behind him now though, he assured himself staunchly. From now on, he would simply revel in being very, very rich and free of all ties. He would not remarry and he would not have a child because ten to one, with his ancestry, he would be a lousy parent.

The police called Lorenzo when he was on the way out to lunch. He froze as the grim facts of the crash were recited. The driver was dead, one of *his* staff. The other passenger was dead. What *other* passenger? he wondered dimly, reeling in shock from what he was hearing. His wife was seriously injured, and he was being advised to get to the hospital as soon as possible. He would visit the driver's family too to offer his condolences, he registered numbly.

His wife? Seriously hurt? The designation shook him inside out because he had already stopped thinking of himself as a husband. But in an emergency, he was Brooke's only relative and if she was hurt, she was entirely *his* responsibility, and no decent human being would think otherwise, he told himself fiercely. Without hesitation, he headed straight to the hospital. He had stopped liking or respecting his wife a long time ago, but he would never have wished any kind of harm on her.

The police greeted him at the hospital, keen to ask what he might know about the other woman, who had died. According to the passport they had found, her name was Milly Taylor, but he had never heard of her before. The police seemed to think that, with it being a wet day, Brooke might have stopped the car to give some random woman a lift, but Lorenzo couldn't imagine Brooke doing anything of that nature and suggested that the unknown woman might be one of

Brooke's social media gurus or possibly a make-up artist or stylist because she frequently hired such people.

He wondered if the accident had been his driver's fault. Consequently, was it *his* fault for continuing to allow Brooke the luxury of a limo with driver? Although the pre-nup Brooke had signed had proved ironclad in protecting his assets and his fortune, Lorenzo had been generous. He had already bought and given Brooke a penthouse apartment in which to live and had hesitated to withdraw the use of the car and driver as well until she had officially moved out of Madrigal Court, his country home. And Brooke had stalled about actually moving out because it suited her to have staff she didn't have to pay making her meals for her and doing the hundred and one things she didn't want to have to do for herself. *Madre di Dio*...what total nonsense was he thinking about at such a grave moment?

The police reassured him that the accident had not been his driver's fault. A foreign truck driver had taken a wrong turn, got into a panic in the heavy traffic and run a set of stop lights, making an accident unavoidable.

Brooke, he learned, had a serious head injury and he was warned by the consultant neurosurgeon about to operate on her that she might not survive. Lorenzo spent the night pacing a bland waiting room, brooding over everything that he had been told. Brooke had facial injuries. The tiny glimpse he'd had of her before she went into surgery, he had found her unrecognisable and he was appalled on her behalf because he had never known a woman whose looks meant more to her. He would engage the very best plastic surgeons to treat her, he promised himself, shame and discomfiture assailing him. As long as she was alive, he would look after her in every way possible, just as if she were *still* a much-loved and cherished wife. That was his bounden duty and he would not be tried and found wanting in a crisis.

When he learned that she had come through the surgery he breathed more freely again. She was in a coma. Only time would tell when she would come out of it or what she would be like when she came round, because such head traumas generally caused further complications and even if she recovered she might be different in some ways, the exhausted surgeon warned him. Furthermore, Brooke was facing a very long and slow recovery process.

He was given her personal effects by a nurse. He recognised her engagement ring, the big solitaire he had slipped on her finger with such love and hope, the matching wedding band he had given her with equal trust and optimism. He swallowed hard, recognising that he was at a crossroads and not at the crossroads of freedom he had expected to become his within weeks. Brooke was his wife and he would look after her and support her in whatever ways were necessary. In the short term, he reflected tautly, he would put the divorce on hold until she was on the road to recovery and capable of expressing her own wishes again.

CHAPTER TWO

THE WOMAN IN the bed was drifting weightless in a cocoon, her awareness coming to her in weird broken flashes.

She heard voices but she didn't recognise them. She heard sounds like bells, buzzes, and bleeps but she didn't recognise them either. And she couldn't move, no matter how hard she strained her will to shift a finger, wriggle a toe or even open her eyes. Her body felt as heavy as lead. And then she heard one voice and, although she didn't recognise it either, she clung to it in her disorientation as though it were a lifeline.

It was a man's voice, deep and dark and measured. It made her listen but at first she couldn't distinguish the words, and even when she began picking up stray words she couldn't string them together into a coherent sentence or think about what the words meant. Maybe it was a television, she thought, wondering why it was constantly tuned to a foreign channel because early on she identified a faint but very definite foreign accent that stroked along his vowel sounds like silk, sometimes softening them, sometimes harshening them. Time had no meaning for her while she listened to the voice.

And then there was the music that came and went in the background. It was the sort of music she had never listened to before, mainly classical. But occasionally she heard birdsong or the surge of waves on the shore or even noises she imagined might be heard in a jungle, as if someone had compiled a diverse sound collection just for her. She loved the birdsong because it made her feel that if she could only try a little harder to wake up, she would waken to a fresh new day.

Lorenzo studied his wife while he stood at the window of her room. Superficially, if one discounted all the machinery and the tubes, Brooke looked as though she were simply asleep, her cascade of white-blonde curls tumbling off the side of the bed in a glorious curtain. They called her, 'the sleeping beauty' in the high-tech care home he had moved her to when the hospital could do no more. She had moved from the coma into a vegetative state and there was no sign of recovery after fifteen months.

Fifteen months, Lorenzo conceded, driving a long-fingered hand through his luxuriant black hair, for fifteen crisis-ridden months, his life had revolved around her treatment. Fifteen months during which she had been in and out of Intensive Care, in and out of surgery, both major and minor, and now she was repaired, broken limbs mended, cuts and bruises healed, her face restored by the very best surgeons and daily physiotherapy keeping her muscles from wasting...but still, she wasn't *fixed*.

Fixing her every problem, banishing the physical damage caused by the accident and readying her for a return to the living had kept Lorenzo going, even when the hopes of the medical staff had begun to fade. He could not let her go, he could *not* allow those machines to be switched off, not while there was hope, and he was fortunate that he was wealthy enough to fly in specialists from round the world, only unfortunately all of them had different opinions on Brooke's prospects of recovery. He had never been humble but it was finally beginning to dawn on Lorenzo that he was not omnipotent and that she might *never* be fixed and might never open her eyes again.

He sat down by the bed and scored a forefinger over the back of her still hand. Her nails were polished, just as her hair was regularly washed and styled. They had wanted to cut her hair short but he had simply brought in a hairdresser to take care of it instead, just as he had brought in nail technicians. It was what Brooke would've wanted, although he had told the hairdresser to stop straightening her hair and leave the natural curls. He knew she would never have agreed to that change and if he accidentally brushed a hand through those glorious tumbling white-blonde ringlets he felt guilt pierce him.

'I *did* love you once,' Lorenzo said almost defiantly in the silent room.

And a finger twitched. Lorenzo froze and studied her hand, which remained in the same position, and he told himself he

had imagined that movement. It wouldn't
be the first time that he had imagined such
a thing and he was being fanciful.

It bothered him that Brooke was so alone
and that he was her sole visitor aside of the
occasional specialists. He had never realised
how isolated she was until after the accident when paparazzi had tried to sneak in
and catch pictures of her but not one single friend had shown up. There had only
been cursory phone calls from her agent
and various other people engaged in building her career and those enquiries had soon
fallen off once the news that she was in a
coma spread. The fame she had gloried in
had, sadly, proved fleeting. There had been
a burst of headlines and speculation in the
wake of the crash but now she seemed to be
forgotten by everyone but him.

Early the following morning, alarm bells
rang and lights flashed from the machinery by the bed. The woman came awake
and went into panic, eyes focusing on an
unfamiliar room and then on the arrival of
two nurses, their faces both concerned and
excited at the same time. She clawed at the

breathing tube in her throat because she couldn't speak and the women tried to both restrain and soothe her, telling her over and over again that the doctor was coming, everything would be all right and that there was nothing to worry about. She thought they were crazy. Her body wouldn't move. She could only move one hand and her arm felt as if it didn't belong to her. How could she possibly have nothing to worry about? Why were they talking nonsense? Did they think she was stupid?

The panic kept on clawing at her, even after the doctor arrived and the breathing tube was removed. He kept on asking her questions, questions she couldn't answer until she couldn't hide from the truth any longer. She didn't *know* who she was. What was her name? She didn't *know* why she was lying in a hospital bed. She didn't have a last memory to offer because her mind was a blank, a complete blank. It was a ridiculous relief to receive an approving nod when she evidently got the name of the Prime Minister right and contrived to name colours correctly.

'What happened to me?' she whispered brokenly, her breath rasping. 'Have I been ill?'

'You were in an accident.' The doctor paused there, exchanging a glance with the staff surrounding the bed.

'What's my name?' she asked shakily.

'Your name is Brooke… Brooke Tassini.'

The name meant absolutely nothing to her, didn't even sound slightly familiar.

'Your husband will be here very soon.'

Brooke's eyes widened to their fullest extent in shock. *I have a husband?*

For some reason, the nurses smiled. 'Oh, yes, you have a husband.'

'A very handsome husband,' one of the women added.

Brooke stared down at her bare wedding finger. She was married. Oh, my goodness, she was married. Did she have children? she asked. No…no children as far as they knew, they said, and a tinge of relief threaded through the panic she was only just holding at bay. Then she felt guilty about that sense of relief. She liked children, *didn't she*? But it was scary enough to have a husband she didn't remember—it would be simply appalling if she had contrived to forget her children as well.

Lorenzo stood outside in the corridor studying the middle-aged doctor babbling at him. And it *was* babble because the care-home staff were not accustomed to their comatose patients waking up and excitement laced with frank worry had taken over.

'It's post-traumatic amnesia, perfectly understandable after a serious head injury. You need someone more qualified than me in the psychiatric field to advise you on her condition, but I would warn you not to tell her anything that might upset her more at the moment. I wouldn't mention yet that other people died in the accident or that you were…er…splitting up at the time of the crash,' the doctor muttered hurriedly, visibly uncomfortable with getting that personal. 'She's in a very high state of stress as it is. Try to calm her, try to keep it upbeat without divulging too much information.'

Lorenzo had been in an early board meeting when the phone call came. He had been so shocked by the news that Brooke had recovered consciousness that he had walked out without a word of explanation. Now that he was on the brink of speaking to her again, he was, for once, at a loss. Brooke didn't *remember* him? Could he believe that of a woman willing to use anything and everything to create a furore in the media? What better way to spring back into the public eye than with an interesting story to tell? When he had first met her, such suspicion would have been foreign to him and momentarily he was furious that he had to consider that she could be faking it. But he had learned the hard way that Brooke was a skilled deceiver.

The door opened and Brooke froze against the pillows, her chest tightening as she snatched in a breath. And there he was in the doorway and there was nothing familiar about him. Indeed, it immediately occurred to her that no normal woman could possibly have forgotten such a man.

He stood well over six feet tall, wide-shouldered, lean of hip and long of leg, and he wore a dark pinstriped suit with a blue tie and white shirt. And he was, undeniably, absolutely breathtaking in the looks department. His hair was black and cropped short and it was the sort of thick springy hair that a woman wanted to run her fingers through. His bronzed features were all high cheekbones and interesting hollows, dissected by a narrow blade of a nose, while his wide sensual mouth was accentuated by the faint dark shadow of stubble surrounding it. His eyes, deep set and very dark and framed with lashes lush as black fans, were even more arresting and resting on her now with a piercing gleam. She could feel her skin heating because that appraisal could have stripped paint.

No, he *couldn't* be her husband, she decided immediately. He had to be some sleek, highly qualified consultant come to suss her out. Instinct seemed to be telling her that her husband would be a much more ordinary sort, maybe a bit homely, a bit tousled, but when his wife woke up after being in a coma, he would, at least, be smiling with relief and happiness. This guy didn't look as if he smiled very often. He was downright intimidating even in the way he stood there, radiating raw masculinity and authority.

'Brooke...' he murmured without any expression at all, walking in and shutting the door behind him and then those amazing eyes were locking to her again and it was a challenge to breathe. 'How are you feeling?'

Her heart was hammering so hard with nerves she felt her throat close over, her already sore throat, still tender from the removal of the breathing tube. But when he spoke, she froze in wonderment because his voice was familiar. 'I know your voice… I *know* your voice!' she gasped with a sense of attainment. 'In fact it's the first thing I've recognised since I woke up…but I don't recognise you. Who are you?'

'Lorenzo Tassini.'

'I'm *married* to *you*?' Brooke yelped in open disbelief.

Lorenzo's brows drew together. He was trying very hard not to stare at her because she was a vision of natural beauty, this woman he had married who had only shown him the ugliness she kept hidden on the inside. With her dishevelled hair hanging across her shoulders, framing her entrancing heart-shaped face, and those huge incredible dark blue, verging-on-violet eyes, she looked utterly angelic. And different, startlingly different, because he didn't think he had ever seen Brooke without her cosmetic enhancements. Brooke would climb out of bed at dawn to put her make-up on, no matter how often he had told her she didn't need it to look good.

But, of course, there were differences in her appearance. She was thinner, for a start, painfully thin in spite of the nourishing diet she had been fed by tube. She looked frail and somehow younger. The surgeons had restored her to perfection, but his acute gaze had already spotted the changes. Her mouth seemed a little wider, a little lusher in its pout, her nose shorter, less defined, and her eyes, those beautiful violet eyes were as bright and inquisitive as a bird's. And he had never ever seen such an expression on Brooke's face before. Brooke rarely showed emotion of any kind but, right now, he was seeing uncertainty, shock and intense curiosity fleeing across her face and it was a novelty for him to be able to interpret her feelings.

'Yes, you're married to me,' he confirmed flatly, recalling the doctor's warning, striving to abide by it when his conscience wanted him to throw the truth out there and be damned for it because he wanted no more lies between them. But if he told her about the divorce, he would lose her trust, her ability to depend on him, and she *needed* him right now. She needed to trust that he would not harm her and that she could rely on him because he knew there was no one else to take his place.

Brooke swallowed painfully and closed her eyes. A headache was beginning to pulse behind her brow. She was ridiculously tired for someone who had only been awake for a couple of hours.

'Would you like a drink?' Lorenzo prompted, lifting the glass with the straw in it.

'Yes…thanks.' Her eyes flickered open again and she sucked eagerly on the straw, the cool water easing her throat. 'I've got so many questions.'

'We'll answer them one by one.'

'But why don't I remember *you* when I remember your voice?' she exclaimed in frustration. 'How long have I been here? Nobody would tell me.'

'You've been here over a year.' Lorenzo

watched her eyes round in further disbelief and once again savoured the newness of being able to read her face. 'After the first few weeks, when you failed to come out of it, the prognosis wasn't optimistic, so it is a source of great satisfaction for me to see you awake.'

'It *is*?' Brooke repeated, brightening in receipt of that acknowledgement. 'Then why don't you show it?'

'*Show* it?' He frowned.

'Smile, look happy. You walked in here looking like the Grim Reaper,' she told him, reddening at her boldness in being that blunt. 'I feel so alone here.'

Ramming his ever-present doubts about Brooke's veracity to the back of his mind, Lorenzo closed a hand over her limp fingers. 'But you're not alone.'

'Sit down beside me…here, on the bed,' she heard herself urge.

He looked as startled as if she had suggested he get into the bed with her and she stiffened in mortification. Instead of doing as she asked, he backed away and sank into the chair by the window. He was very reserved, she decided, adding to her first impression of him, not a guy who relaxed or who was easy with informality. It was impossible to imagine that she had ever been in bed with him and, at the thought, her face burned.

'How long have we been married?' she pressed.

'Three years now.'

Then, she had *definitely* been in bed with him, Brooke realised, and she would have squirmed with embarrassment had she had the ability to move normally. But nothing was normal about her body or her brain throwing up random embarrassing thoughts, she conceded ruefully, and nothing was normal about their situation either, and it had to be causing Lorenzo equal discomfort that he had a wife who didn't remember him.

'I'm sorry about all this. I'm sorry I don't know you and that I've caused you all this trouble.'

'You haven't caused me any trouble whatsoever,' Lorenzo lied, wondering what was wrong with her because Brooke's view of the world was generally one-sided. She didn't consider other people or their needs. She valued those around her strictly in accordance with the benefits they could bring her. She could be charm personified to get what she wanted but would then dispense with a person's services the instant she achieved her objective. But, of course, he reminded himself darkly, he *was* valuable to Brooke at this precise moment when she had nobody else to fall back on.

'It's kind of you to say that but all these months I've been lying here like a rock and I must've been the most awful worry for you,' she mumbled, her words slurring.

'I think you need to rest now,' Lorenzo told her, rising from his seat. 'I need to make arrangements for you to be moved to a more suitable facility where you can convalesce.'

Her head heavy, she turned her eyes back to him. 'I just want to go home,' she whispered weakly.

'I'm afraid that's not an option. Right now, you need a rehabilitation programme to regain your strength and medical support to deal with your amnesia,' Lorenzo explained smoothly.

'How did we meet?' she muttered drowsily, her brain spinning on and on, in spite of her exhaustion, wanting answers to countless questions.

'At a party in Nice. I was there on business.'

'You're a businessman?' she slurred.

'A banker,' he advanced.

'I don't like banks,' she mumbled, and then thought in surprise, Where did that thought come from?

Brows pleating, Lorenzo paused at the door to look back at her searchingly. 'Why don't you like banks?'

With an enormous effort she opened her eyes again and there he was, standing directly below the lights, his hair blue-black, his eyes transformed into liquid-gold pools of enquiry. He looked devastatingly handsome and she smiled at him sleepily. 'I don't know. It was just a random thought that came out of nowhere,' she admitted.

'Go to sleep, Brooke,' he urged. 'I'll see you tomorrow.'

'No kiss goodbye?'

Lorenzo froze at what struck him as an almost childlike question, which was laughable, he told himself, for anyone acquainted with Brooke's past history. 'No kiss. You're too sleepy and I like my women awake.'

'That's mean,' she mumbled.

Lorenzo stood at the foot of the bed watching her sleep. He should've been on the phone looking into convalescent facilities. He should've been seeking out a top psychiatrist to treat her. He should've told her that he wouldn't see her tomorrow because he was flying to Milan for an international banking conference. But he did none of those sensible things. He stood and he watched her sleep, feeling guilty at leaving her but all the while thinking in rampant disbelief that he might have married Brooke, but suddenly he was feeling as though he didn't know *her* either. Everyone had layers, he told himself irritably. Maybe this was how Brooke was when she was unsure of herself and no longer knew who she was. Restored to her fantastic wardrobe and her make-up and her headlines, she would once again become the woman he remembered.

Brooke sank into a seat in front of Mr Selby, her psychiatrist, and stowed the stick she was using. After a physio session she was always very sore and the slight limp she still had made her clumsy as she tired towards the end of the day, but she didn't complain because just being able to walk again felt like a precious enough gift.

'How have you been over the last few days?' the psychiatrist enquired over the top of his eccentric half-moon glasses.

'Great, but no flashes, no memories yet,' she said uneasily. 'Everything still feels so strange. Lorenzo brought me this giant metal case of cosmetics to replace the one that was destroyed in the accident and I think he was expecting me to be ecstatic, but I couldn't identify half the stuff in the box. I used a bit of it for his next visit. I didn't want him to think his present was a disappointment.'

'You seem to care about Lorenzo a great deal,' her companion remarked.

'Surely that's healthy when I'm married to him?' Brooke replied.

'Of course, you've been forced to depend on him, but it will be even more healthy for you to embrace a little independence as you recover your physical strength.'

Brooke's nod of acknowledgement was stiff. Over the past two months, she had learned just to let advice she didn't relish pass over her head. Everyone she met in the rehabilitation centre seemed to want to give her advice. She had dealt with surprise after surprise since her arrival. She had discovered that she was married to an extremely wealthy man and piece by piece she had learned that, before the crash, she had been a minor celebrity, a known fashion icon and often a source of media interest.

Those revelations hadn't felt natural to her and hadn't seemed to fit in very well with the quieter, less confident image she had slowly been developing of herself. But when she asked Lorenzo when she could go on the Internet to research her own previous life, he had insisted that it would be the wrong thing to do and that her memories would have a much better chance of returning if they weren't forced.

'What will I do if the memories never come back?'

'You will rebuild yourself. You've been very lucky. Your injury was severe, but you have no other ongoing problems,' Mr Selby reminded her bracingly.

Except a husband she *still* couldn't remember, a reality that tormented Brooke every time he visited her. But he wasn't able to visit her as often as he had hoped because he was an exceptionally busy banker, who went abroad several times a month. And her initial impression of Lorenzo had been spot on in its accuracy. He *was* very reserved. He rarely touched her in even the most fleeting way. It was a little as though she had an invisible force field around her, she conceded with a regretful grimace. Obviously he was deeply uncomfortable with the fact that she didn't remember him but his hands-off approach wasn't helping her to feel any closer to him. It was a subject she needed to tackle…and soon, she told herself ruefully.

He hadn't walked away while she was in a coma, so why was he keeping his distance now? Did he love her? Did he still find her attractive? Or was their marriage in trouble?

She agonised over the options in the giant box of make-up because he was coming to see her that evening. She even leafed through the totally impractical garments he had had brought to her, which hung in the wardrobe, and selected a dress because greeting Lorenzo in the yoga pants that she wore for physio sessions hadn't got her any-where. Lorenzo was used to a fashion queen, so she would strive to please and maybe that would warm him up.

Her skin heating at that enterprising thought, she did her face and put on the electric-blue dress that she thought was hideously bright, almost noon in shade, but presumably she had bought it and liked it once. She slid into it and then embarked on the matching shoes. She wasn't supposed to wear heels yet but she wouldn't be mov-ing around much, which was just as well because the shoes pinched painfully at the toes.

Lorenzo stepped out of his chauffeur-driven limo and studied the modern building with disfavour as he braced himself for another visit to his wife. If she didn't recover her memories soon, he was likely to be forced to the point of telling her the truth about their marriage. And the psychiatrist had warned him that Brooke wasn't ready to deal with that reality, that he had become her 'safe place' and if that support was suddenly withdrawn, it might well disrupt her fragile mental state and send her hurtling back into panic mode, which would set back the recovery process.

He was already in major conflict with his lawyers' warnings. They didn't take a humane approach to the situation he was in, merely cautioning him that frequent visits to his estranged wife would only convince a judge that granting him a divorce would get in the way of what could be viewed as a potential reconciliation. And he didn't want to do that, no, he definitely did not *want* to stay married to Brooke. There had to be a hard limit to his compassion and care. But that wasn't what was really bothering him, was it?

He wanted her: that was the *real* problem. In fact, he lusted after her more, it seemed, than he had ever lusted after her. Why? Because she was different, *so* different he couldn't believe it sometimes and, quite ridiculously, he *liked* her now. How was that possible? Logic told him that he was seeing Brooke as she might have been before the lust for fame and the infatuation with her own beauty had taken hold of her. Even more shockingly, Brooke *au naturel* was a class act.

Only he didn't *think* it was an act any longer because he was convinced that the woman he remembered could never ever have carried off that outstanding mix of artless naivety and innocence she showed him. In short, Brooke was all sorts of things she had never been before with him...caring, unselfish, undemanding. She had made him like her again, but he was determined not to be sucked back into that swamp a second time, he reminded himself grimly. She was recovering well and soon he would be able to cut their ties again and slot her into that penthouse apartment.

Lorenzo strode in and Brooke leapt upright at speed, wanting him to see that she had made the effort, wanting him to see that she was truly getting back to normal...*and* ready to go home.

'You look...more like yourself this evening,' Lorenzo commented as she regarded him expectantly.

Her violet eyes, bright with what he recognised as excitement, unsettled him.

'I think I'm ready to leave here...to come

home,' she told him urgently. 'I'm sure it would be better for me to be in a familiar place. They're very kind to me here but I'm going crazy cooped up like this and it's so boring and uneventful. Your visits are the only highlights in my week.'

With difficulty, Lorenzo mastered his consternation. 'I'll speak to your doctors tomorrow. We don't want to rush into anything. After all, you couldn't even walk two months ago.'

'I'm getting stronger every day!' Brooke argued. 'Why don't you see that?'

'I *do* see it,' Lorenzo countered levelly. 'But until you recover your memory, it's too risky.'

Brooke's hands coiled into tight fists, the sudden burst of temper that ignited inside her an explosion of the frustration she had been fighting off for days. 'Am I going to stay here for ever, then, as a patient?' she exclaimed angrily. 'Because I've already been told, and you must also know, that I might *never* get my memory back!'

Lorenzo gritted his teeth. He did know that, but he had confidently put the warning to the back of his mind because every time he saw her, he expected to see her change back into the woman he remembered. 'Sit down,' he urged. 'We'll discuss this calmly.'

Brooke dropped down on the side of the bed. Lorenzo studied her. She had been all built up to ask him to take her home and now she was upset, and he felt as if he was being cruel even though he knew that he had no other choice. Sitting there, she was a picture with her tangled ringlets half concealing her piquant face, the faint pout of her luscious pink mouth, the long length of her legs displayed to perfection in that dress and those shoes. A punch of lust tightened his groin and he tensed, willing back his desire, fighting for control. The yoga pants had driven him crazy, showing every curve, every indent, but Lorenzo wasn't easily tempted, not where Brooke was concerned, and he had fought that reaction every rigorous step of the way. He stood by the window gazing out at the tranquil courtyard garden in the centre of the building, striving to calm himself.

'Before the accident...' Brooke began hesitantly. 'Our marriage was in trouble, wasn't it?'

At that moment she didn't want the positive answer she suspected to be her new reality. Even so, she felt she still had to ask and had to be strong enough to confront such an unwelcome truth because, in that scenario, pretending wasn't fair to either of them.

Disconcerted, Lorenzo froze in position. 'What makes you think that?' he enquired in a deliberately mild tone.

'It doesn't take a rocket scientist,' she framed a little unevenly. 'You never touch me unless you can't avoid it. You never mention anything personal and if I ask questions in that line you stall. You don't want me home either. Just be honest, Lorenzo. I *can* take it. And then, just go home or back to the bank because you seem to work eighteen hours a day.'

Lorenzo almost ground his teeth in frustration. It would have been the perfect moment to speak had he not had to consider her condition. He glanced across at her and saw the tears shimmering like sunshine on water in her eyes.

Angrily aware of the tears prickling, Brooke dashed them away with an impatient hand. 'Stop treating me like a child, stop choosing your words. I'm twenty-eight years old, for goodness' sake, not a little girl! It's bad enough not remembering stuff, but it's a *torment* to be sitting here wondering all the time what sort of relationship we have…'

In disconcertion, Lorenzo strode forward just as she leapt up in haste, determined not to cry in front of him. 'Just go home!' she told him fiercely as she headed for the door and the sanctuary of the patients' lounge. 'I'll see you another day—'

But she tried to move too fast in the high heels and her weaker leg flailed and tipped her over. She was within inches of crashing down painfully on the hard floor when Lorenzo snatched her up, lifting her clean off her tottering feet and settling her down in front of him in the circle of his arms. The scent of him that close was like an aphrodisiac to her senses, an inner clenching down in her pelvis instantly responding. She closed her arms round his neck because she had decided that if he couldn't even kiss her, obviously he no longer felt attracted to her, and she would get her answer to how he felt about her one way or another.

Lorenzo collided with her wonderfully unusual eyes and, involuntarily, he bent down and kissed her, damning himself for even that momentary surrender. But he was too clever by half with women not to guess that she was giving him the green light to test him. One brief kiss and nobody was catching it on camera, he reminded himself, and then her soft, succulent mouth opened invitingly under his and suddenly all bets were off because the taste of her went to his head and his groin like a bushfire licking out of control.

She tasted like…she tasted like… His primal nature threatened to take over, almost made him forget that since she had lost her memory this was their *first* kiss as far as she was concerned. Quite deliberately he tried to rein himself back. But Brooke was still blown off her feet by the explosion of passion Lorenzo delivered with his mouth. His lips were hard and urgent and demanding, somehow everything she had been craving without realising it for endless weeks, and he crushed her to his tall, powerful frame.

It was off-the-charts exciting.

Her hands bit into his broad shoulders to keep her upright while the intoxicating chemistry of his mouth on hers left her breathless and dizzy and afflicted with all sorts of reactions that felt entirely new to her. Of course, they couldn't be new to her, but her heart was racing and her nipples became tight and almost sore in their sensitivity beneath her clothes. At the apex of her thighs, there was a burn, a sort of pulsing ache that inflamed her senses and, against her abdomen, she could feel the literal effect she was having on Lorenzo as well and somehow that shocked her when it shouldn't have done.

Indeed, for Brooke, Lorenzo's sizzling kiss was the first true gift she had had in all the weeks of her frustrating convalescence while she worried and wondered about who she truly was and wondered even harder how Lorenzo wanted her to behave. She was in constant conflict, struggling between what little she knew about her past self and the newer and equally unknown self that often prompted her to behave differently. But that kiss restored her equilibrium. It was *acceptance*, it was proof positive that her husband *still* wanted her and that she had been fretting herself into a state about nothing.

As he lowered Brooke down onto the bed

and broke their connection with a slight shudder of recoil, Lorenzo was reminded very much of a saying a teacher of his had been fond of recounting to him: 'between a rock and a hard place'. 'Damned if you do, damned if you don't,' struck him as more apt. Still, what was one kiss? he reasoned wrathfully, instantly going into damage-limitation mode and stepping back from her. He was awesomely aware of the arousal he couldn't hide below the finely tailored trousers, the coolness he couldn't yet slide into place, and so furious with himself for succumbing to her again that his lean brown hands clenched into fists.

Lorenzo had once liked to pride himself on being an unemotional man like his late father but the unemotional man who had married Brooke had discovered otherwise. He had felt *tortured* by the endless dramas and he had shut that weak and disturbing part of himself away again, closed it down, re-embraced his calm, his control, his...sanity. He wasn't going back there, no, not even for the sake of honour or decency!

'That was wonderful.' Brooke gave him a huge smile, utterly impervious to his feelings at that moment. 'I feel so much better about us.'

'Good,' Lorenzo gritted between his perfect teeth, because it felt like another nail in his coffin that she had come alive in his arms as she never had before. He was in shock, he conceded, acknowledging the fact that Brooke had never kissed him back that way in their entire acquaintance, had never shown him an atom of the desire he had assumed she had for him when he married her. He shook his handsome dark head slightly as though to clear it. She was *so* different, but hadn't the doctors warned him of that possibility?

He trained his dark deep gaze on her. 'I'm not an emotional man, Brooke.'

'You don't really need to tell me that. It's kind of obvious,' Brooke pointed out. 'You've never shown me any emotion in your visits and it worried me about us but obviously we managed to get married anyway and right now I can see how tense you are.'

Lorenzo was starting to feel like the accused in the dock. 'I'm not tense,' he insisted.

But the tension was engraved in his lean, darkly handsome features, Brooke recognised with relief. Lorenzo might be locked up tight in his reserve, but he had shown her wonderfully strong emotion in that kiss... *hadn't he*? Or had that only been sexual hunger? And why didn't she know the difference? The way she seemed to just know other things? Like the names of the seasons, the days of the week? She swallowed hard, afraid to get carried away by her expectations of him, afraid to expect too much.

'Will you bring me home this week?' she just asked him baldly. 'I'm ready even if the doctors fuss about the idea. I can't stay here for ever...unless that's what you'd prefer?'

That anxious question shot through Lorenzo much like a whip because he could see the stress and the level of concern she was trying, very poorly, to hide from him, and he marvelled all over again at the complete absence of her once unrevealing shuttered expressions. 'Of course not,' he responded by rote. 'I'll speak to them.'

Content to have received that response, Brooke slid off the bed and walked over to him. 'I won't be any trouble to anyone. It's not like I'm depressed or mentally troubled in some way. I've only lost my memory. I just want my life…' *and* my husband, she added inwardly, 'back.'

Suddenly, Lorenzo found himself smiling at the almost enthralling prospect of reuniting Brooke with her wardrobe, her jewellery and her precious scrapbooks and files of headlines and articles. Nothing surely was more likely to revive her memory than her possessions and her media triumphs? What the hell had he hoped to achieve when he kept her in a sterile medical environment? Deprived of everything she valued and enjoyed in life? Nothing in the private clinic was familiar to her and nothing here would appeal to her tastes. In such a place there was no stimulation that could help her to recover her memory. *Sì*… He would take her to her supposed home and in all likelihood she would recover there and remember that she hated him. He could bear a few more weeks—*couldn't he?*

Even more enchanted by his rare smile, Brooke went pink. She had virtually thrown herself at him and, while it had taken a lot of initiative to act that way with him and had felt horribly pushy, the ploy had indisputably worked. As long as she didn't mention their marriage or love or anything of that nature, Lorenzo could handle it, but for the first time she was questioning what in their marriage or in his background had made him so uncomfortable about ordinary feelings.

CHAPTER THREE

IN THE LIMOUSINE that wafted her down the long driveway towards the giant building that sat at the bottom, Brooke sat wide-eyed with wonder but striving to conceal the fact. It seemed that she was married to a man who was very much wealthier than she had understood, and that was a shock too. But acting shocked got old quickly and she was slowly trying to learn how to school her face into less revealing reactions every time she got a surprise about herself. This was *her* life, after all, she reminded herself soothingly, *her* home.

And Madrigal Court was gorgeous, she thought helplessly, as the sunlight glinted off the rows of windows and the old brick with its intricate designs and so many chimneys—a country house that must've been hundreds of years old. Tudor? she wondered with a frown, disconcerted to find that term popping up in the back of her brain. Seemingly she knew more about old buildings than she had assumed, or could it have been a memory? She was desperate to recall something concrete: an event, an image, a face, a fact, anything really, she acknowledged ruefully, but so far there had been nothing and that had to be incredibly frustrating for Lorenzo.

Without even thinking about it, she reached for his hand because she had been so very flattered that he had taken a day off to share her homecoming with her. She was extremely conscious that he worked very hard and for very long hours and she thought that might have been why she had concentrated equally hard, it seemed, to make a separate role and career for herself. Clearly, Lorenzo had married a strong, independent and confident woman and Brooke was desperately trying to shore up those traits in herself.

There would be no clinging, no whinging, when he disappeared abroad for days at a time, no mention of the truth that she missed him terribly when he was gone. He wouldn't want to hear that kind of stuff and he would be disappointed in her. And hadn't he had enough disappointment already, sufficient to end many a marriage, she reminded herself, when his wife wakened and didn't know him from a stranger in the street?

Totally shocked by that gesture, Lorenzo flicked a covert black-lashed glance down at their linked hands and breathed in deep and slow to embrace calm. His enthralling vision of her walking into her wardrobe and shrieking in delight, 'I'm home!' still refused to retreat. But this new version of Brooke didn't shriek, and her voice was low-pitched, just one of the many, many changes in her that unsettled him. It was almost as though she had had a personality transplant, he mused. *Per Dio*, she had *cried* when he told her that her parents had passed away before he met her and that she had no other relatives, nobody, who could fill in the blanks of the memory loss she was enduring now. Of course, there might be photos of her family somewhere in Brooke's stuff, he reflected hopefully, because he knew that would please her.

At her request, he had retrieved her wedding ring from the home safe and she had threaded it on as though it were something special, not the plain band that she had originally dismissed as 'not very imaginative'. Nothing that didn't glitter with valuable jewels had once incited Brooke's admiration.

She listened to his advice now as well. She hadn't asked for a phone or even the Internet again, which impressed him as being even more weird, for Brooke had *lived* on her phone. How could she not be missing it? Of course, she didn't know *who* or what she had to miss, did she? Lorenzo's lean bronzed face hardened. Not least the very married film star who had recently had an aide contact Lorenzo to enquire after his wife's health, evidently having heard a rumour that Brooke was recovering from the accident. Lorenzo suspected there had been an affair between them, but he reminded himself that Brooke's sex life was, thankfully, no longer any of his business. They might remain legally married but there was nothing deeper involved.

Brooke walked up the worn stone steps into the house and smiled at the middle-aged man opening the door for their arrival. 'And you are?'

'Stevens, madam,' the older man supplied in surprise.

'Thank you,' she said quietly, moving indoors and stopping dead to take in the big imposing entrance hall made cosy by the low fire burning in the ancient fireplace to one side. 'Oh, this is beautiful!' she claimed, startling Lorenzo.

'You hated this house,' Lorenzo heard himself murmur in soft contradiction. 'You wanted a modern home, a McMansion. I refused to move because this was my mother's family home and, although I never knew her, I enjoyed the knowledge that she had once lived here.'

'*Hated* it?' Brooke exclaimed in disbelief, spinning round to look at him. 'I don't think that's possible.'

Watching her flounder with uncertainty as soon as she had spoken and accepted that such a former attitude was perfectly possible, Lorenzo registered his error in being that honest and at speed he strode over to a door to throw it wide. 'Lots of married couples have different tastes.' He dismissed that hint of contention smoothly. 'This room is more your style.'

What style? Brooke almost asked for every piece of furniture was gilded and the drapes, the upholstery and even the carpet were pristine white. Even the vase of flowers on the low table was filled with white blooms. In her opinion, it was stark and uninviting, but it certainly gave a striking effect.

'And this is you...' Lorenzo indicated the large professional photograph on the wall in which she posed on the same sofa for a *Dream House* magazine interview she had, according to him, given only weeks before the accident.

Brooke stared in fascination at the woman in the photograph and her fingers went up to pluck uneasily at her loose ringlets as she studied that smooth straight fall of hair in the image. 'I should be straightening my hair!' she gasped suddenly.

'I like it natural,' Lorenzo dared to impart.

'Honestly?' she queried tautly as she stared at that flawlessly groomed, almost inhumanly perfect image with a sinking heart. It was undeniably her, but it was *not* the version of her that she was currently providing him with.

'Honestly.'

In that moment, Brooke felt overwhelmed. Coming home was proving more of a challenge than she had expected. Was it possible that the head injury had altered her tastes? She supposed it was. When she had expressed her concern about such changes to Mr Selby, he had been very reassuring, never failing to remind her that she was lucky to be alive and relatively unscathed as if the loss of her every memory from childhood was something she simply had to accept. And perhaps it was, and there was nothing less attractive than self-pity, she told herself fiercely, moving back into the hall.

'Let's go upstairs,' Lorenzo urged. 'I'll show you your room.'

Your room, Brooke noted. 'Don't we share?'

Lorenzo cast her a lazy, careless smile because he was fully rehearsed on that answer. 'You like your own space and you often took your stylist up there to decide on outfits. Sharing wasn't practical.'

'You know more about my life than I

know about yours,' Brooke couldn't help commenting.

'I don't think that there's anything in the world of finance that would interest you,' Lorenzo parried. 'Unless, of course, you've decided to set up a business or something of that nature.'

'Not just at the minute, no,' she quipped, breathing in deep.

So, separate bedrooms, little wonder Lorenzo was so physically detached from her and prone to treating her as though she were a friend rather than a wife. Even though they lived in an enormous house, they didn't seem to share much as a couple. Not a bed, not taste, not their lives. It was unhealthy but perhaps Lorenzo liked his marriage that way even if it didn't appeal to her, she ruminated worriedly. How had she let the man she loved move so far from her in every way?

Obviously she loved him. She couldn't believe that she would have married him for any other reason. His money, his giant house and his servants all made her feel intimidated. But *he* didn't intimidate her, he made her…happy. Mr. Selby had urged her to think about whether or not that was just her insecurity talking and had asked her how she could possibly still love a man she didn't remember. But she knew that she did in the same way she knew that the sun would rise in the morning. She had remembered Lorenzo's voice and it was the *only* thing she remembered, which to her signified and proved his overwhelming importance in her life.

Brooke walked into another blindingly white room, but this time it was a bedroom and she decided that the absence of colour did give a certain feel of tranquillity.

'And then there's your favourite place,' Lorenzo proclaimed, casting wide another door.

Brooke froze on the threshold of an amazing dressing room. But it was so big, so packed with stuff it didn't really qualify for that description. Racks and racks of shoes and bags lined the walls in glass cabinets. Rails and rails of zingy, colourful garments hung in readiness. It was a feast of conspicuous consumerism, a rebuttal of the 'less is more' mentality, and she thought, Oh, dear heaven, I'm greedy and extravagant and spoilt rotten! And then a calmer voice switched on inside her, reminding her that being a fashion icon had sort of been her job. She forced herself deeper into the room to browse through the clothes, hoping for something to jar her memory, glancing at labels and surprised that she only recognised the household names of famous designers that everyone knew. In the general knowledge sense, her fashion antenna seemed to be running on an empty tank.

'Of course, you'll have to throw it all out.'

Brooke whirled, violet eyes huge. *'Throw it out?'* she gasped incredulously.

'Because everything in here is old and out of fashion now.' Lorenzo tossed out that award-winning lure with deep satisfaction because he had already worked out how best to occupy his soon-to-be ex-wife. 'Your wardrobe is out of date. You'll need to start from scratch again and replace it all.'

'But that would be horribly wasteful,' Brooke framed in disbelief, fingering through a rack of jeans, searching for an ordinary pair but finding only slashed, sparkly or embroidered ones, marvelling that her former self had apparently never succumbed to a desire to simply wear something comfortable.

'It's the way that you live.' Lorenzo shrugged, brilliant, thickly lashed dark eyes cynical and assured. 'Every season you start again, so I imagine you'll be shopping until you drop for weeks.'

Brooke nodded jerkily since it seemed to be what he expected from her. 'It seems a very extravagant way to live,' she remarked uneasily.

'I can well afford extravagant,' Lorenzo intoned, wondering why she wasn't one bit excited at the prospect of shopping, wondering why she looked kind of lost standing there in the middle of the room, rather like a little girl contemplating a giant dress-up box that frightened her. This was Brooke's world, from the fashion magazines piled on the coffee table to the immaculate shoe collection. And she *didn't* recognise any of it, he acknowledged grimly.

At least now, she could explore her life, Brooke reminded herself, for there had to be personal things tucked away somewhere within the two rooms, surely photos of her late parents and that kind of stuff, she reasoned as Lorenzo departed. As for the fashion end of things, she clearly wasn't able to become a fashion icon again in her current state of mind and she would just have to move on from that and find something else to keep her busy. Reinventing yourself was all the rage these days, she reminded herself dully. It was not as though she had a choice when she couldn't imagine wearing a see-through lace dress or jeans that exposed her bottom cheeks.

That reflection, however, threw yet another obstacle into her path. Almost certainly that more audacious woman was the woman Lorenzo knew and had chosen to marry. Brooke paled at that acknowledgement. A *sexier* woman. Was that the common denominator at the heart of her marriage? That together sexier Brooke and more reserved Lorenzo meshed like magnets? Was that why Lorenzo was now so distant with her? Because she wasn't putting out the right vibes any longer with her clothing and her manner? Well, she was just going to have to fake it, wasn't she?

What do you know about being sexy? she asked herself limply. But she had to *know* those things to make such daring clothing choices! She relived that kiss and a slow burn reignited low in her pelvis and she shifted restlessly. Maybe she was sexier in bed than she imagined and when it happened it would all just come seamlessly together for her...but what if it didn't? What if her apparent stock of general knowledge didn't include the bedroom stuff? What if she lay there like a graven image and freaked him out? And why was she even having these thoughts, she asked herself, when to date even getting a kiss out of Lorenzo had entailed practically falling on him? Maybe *she* was the partner who made all the sexy, inviting moves, she thought anxiously, and if that was true, the onus would be on *her*...

Perhaps Lorenzo had simply been waiting to bring her home, she reasoned, and tonight, when she was tucked up in bed, he would visit?

CHAPTER FOUR

'I'D LIKE SOME details about the accident,' Brooke declared over dinner two weeks later.

'I don't think that's a good idea,' Lorenzo informed her lazily.

For the first time ever, Brooke wanted to slap her husband for still treating her like a vulnerable child to be protected from every ill wind. 'I disagree. Since I wasn't driving—I mean, you told me that—who *was* driving?'

'An employee. I'm afraid that he died,' Lorenzo told her smoothly.

Brooke lost colour and stilled. 'Oh, how dreadful! I should go and see his family. Will you give me the address?' she pressed.

'He didn't have a family as such. He lived with an elderly mother. I've ensured that she is financially secure. You don't need to get involved,' Lorenzo assured her.

'I think the least I can do is visit his mother to offer my condolences,' Brooke responded firmly.

Lorenzo almost rolled his eyes at this new caring, sharing display of Brooke's. He compressed his hard mouth. Every time he saw her, she annoyed him by being so beautiful, so...*tempting*. There she sat, hair foaming in ringlets and cascading round her like some cartoon mermaid, triangular face bare of cosmetics, violet eyes bright and friendly and natural and, in truth, she remained drop-dead gorgeous. Yet she was wearing jeans, simple plain jeans, and flat shoes. She was another almost unrecognisable incarnation of Brooke and one he didn't intend to waste time on because the transformation wouldn't, *couldn't* possibly last. Inevitably, her indomitable will, her piranha-fish appetites for sex, media exposure and money would resurface and he, for one, would be a great deal happier.

He didn't want to be reminded of that treacherous kiss in the clinic when he had inexplicably contrived to overlook all the other men she had betrayed him with. Of that kiss, it was enough to recall that she had burned him alive and filled him with a hunger he refused to satisfy. He was even more astonished that she could *still* have that effect on him. Only days before the accident he had enjoyed the definitive proof that he was completely impervious to her looks and her seductive wiles. He could only suppose that being forced into a protective role for so long with his estranged wife had somehow softened his previous hard shell of cold disinterest. After all, he had never been the kind of foolish man who returned to explore his worst mistake and that was what Brooke genuinely was to him: *his worst mistake.*

'Do you want the full story of the accident? Even if it's distressing?' he prompted, reminding himself that keeping such secrets from her wasn't doing anything to help her adapt to her return to the land of the living.

Feeling a little threatened now and worried about what he might have held back from her, Brooke nodded urgently. 'Yes.'

'There was another woman in the limo with you and she died as well. We don't know what she was doing with you because, although I looked into her history before the funeral, I couldn't see anything relevant that would have brought you together that day.'

Brooke's smooth brow furrowed. 'That's a puzzle. Who was she?'

'She was a waitress in a London café, although she'd quit her job that same day, quoting a family emergency, but when I investigated it turned out that she had no family and there was nothing of interest about her,' Lorenzo recounted with a fluid Italian shrug of dismissal. 'I suppose we'll never know what she was doing in the car with you that day unless you regain your memory.'

Brooke was troubled by the discovery that some mystery woman had been with her on the day of the crash. She had already discovered a severe absence of personal possessions in her bedroom. She had waded through a dozen files packed with press clippings and some rather suggestive headlines, depicting her with other men in nightclubs, but she hadn't found a single picture of her parents or indeed of anyone else. Her life, evidently, had been lived solely through the media and nothing else had much mattered to her, and that saddened her because her previous existence now seemed shallow to her and empty of real purpose.

As for her marriage, she ruminated regretfully, it didn't appear to be much healthier than her lifestyle had been because she barely saw Lorenzo except at the dinner table. When she had made the effort to rise at dawn to breakfast with him, he had not seemed remotely appreciative of her company and had buried his nose back in the *Financial Times*, the one and only media publication that came to the house.

It was ironic that she had actually been spending more personal time with her husband when he had been visiting her at the clinic. Now that she was back home, he was perfectly polite and pleasant, but it was almost as if she didn't really exist on his terms, which was weird, *wasn't it?*

But everything was weird in their relationship, she conceded wretchedly. Why didn't he sleep with her? Why didn't he want sex when popular parlance suggested that men always wanted sex? What was wrong with her? Or what was wrong with their marriage? She had tried to ignore the signs that something was not quite right but after a fortnight of being treated like a house guest rather than a wife, Brooke felt that she could no longer disregard suspicions that were a deep source of concern to her. After all, if Lorenzo didn't want her any more, what was she doing living in *his* house? Obviously she could only be uncomfortable with the fear that she wasn't truly welcome below the roof of the place she had mistakenly assumed was her true home.

'Why do you never take me out anywhere with you?' Brooke asked with a directness she had not dared to utilise with Lorenzo before.

Lorenzo glanced up from his plate, beautiful dark deep-set eyes shrewd and level, and she experienced that same maddening little prickling of awareness that his gaze always evoked and her heart started to thump faster inside her tight chest. 'We've always had separate social lives. And, unhappily, if we *are* seen in public together, you would be mobbed by the paparazzi because you are the former beauty maven who has now returned from the dead and many people are very curious about you. I don't like press attention in my private life...however, you do.'

'Oh…' Brooke breathed, crushed by those truths delivered so instantaneously. 'You think there might be headlines?'

'I *know* there would be. Brooke…' Lorenzo sighed and lounged back in his chair, devastatingly good-looking and infuriatingly calm. 'There have been cameras waiting at the foot of the drive to catch a photo of you since the day I brought you home. If you'd even once gone shopping, you would've seen them there. Maybe you don't feel like having that media attention right now?'

'I don't,' she confirmed.

'But it's still a very large part of who you used to be,' Lorenzo reminded her. 'And the paps aren't going to give up and go away any time soon.'

Having dealt that final blow, Lorenzo left for the Tassini Bank while Brooke retired to her white bedroom to read a book she had bought online about Italians, seeking in some small way to redress her ignorance of her husband. But there seemed little point reading about how Italians highly valued their families and seeking such a trait in Lorenzo. He was diligent in assuring that her medical needs were covered with regular online sessions with Mr Selby and physio sessions with a personal trainer, but his care never ever got more personal than that. She was fed, housed, clothed, medicated and that was that.

Along with jeans and casual tops, she had bought a dress, low-necked, short and scarlet in hue, and high heels. She viewed the more decorative fitted outfit as a move forward, a first step in becoming the woman whom Lorenzo obviously expected her to be. Now, sadly, she wasn't even sure she would have the nerve to wear it because he had shut her down again.

Two other people had died in that accident and *she* had survived. She was much luckier than she had ever appreciated, and she knew that her first outing would include a visit to the driver's mother and a respectful call at the cemetery to the grave of the woman who had been with her that day. Maybe she had been a friend, Brooke reflected sadly, for she could hardly have failed to note that she didn't seem to have friends in the way that other women had. Hadn't she liked other women? Hadn't other women liked her? The lack of a friend or relative to turn to sometimes made her feel very alone...

Blasted self-pity, she told herself off firmly, and returned to her book while wondering if she had the nerve to wear that dress for dinner and whether Lorenzo would even notice what she wore, because he didn't seem to look at her that much.

Just then, however, when she was least expecting it, the door literally burst open and she jerked bolt upright on top of the bed, her violet eyes wide with surprise.

The very image of innocence, Lorenzo thought in a rage as he strode across the room to slap the newspaper he had bought for that purpose down on the foot of the bed. The lurid headline ran: *She Doesn't Know Who She Is!*

He was furious with himself most of all for starting to trust her again even though he knew she was a liar and a manipulator. It wasn't like him to lose his temper, but when he had seen that newspaper headline, he had felt betrayed, and then he had wondered *why* he felt betrayed when Brooke was only doing what she had always done in seeking to shape her public image and stoke press interest. He should've been better prepared, should've expected such behaviour from her. It was his own fault that he felt as though she had deceived him. When, after all, had he begun to forget what kind of a woman she was?

'I should've guessed that you'd have your own more direct but *sly* way of dealing with the media!' Lorenzo fired down at her.

Brooke was frozen to the spot in disbelief by his behaviour because Lorenzo had never once raised his voice to her before. But at this moment, he was ferociously angry with her and it showed in every honed, hard lineament of his lean, darkly handsome features. 'Go on…look at the article and tell me you're not responsible for this outrage!' he challenged with contempt.

Trembling, Brooke lifted the tabloid newspaper, shaken to see the photo of her in the blue dress she had worn at the clinic now adorning the front page. She recalled the friendly nurse who had asked if she could take a picture on her phone. Brooke had said yes, had believed that it was the dress that the woman was interested in. She hadn't known enough about safeguarding herself from such exploitation to say, no, sorry, she conceded in dismay. So, it *was* absolutely her fault, just as Lorenzo believed, that that picture was in a newspaper.

'Obviously it was more than your vanity could bear to have the press speculating that you could be scarred or in a wheelchair!' Lorenzo bit out in raw condemnation. 'You tell me you don't want media attention and then you do...*this*? You give an interview to them? *Madre di Dio*, why the hell am I acting surprised?'

'An interview?' she whispered, turning the page with shaking fingers, intimidated more than she liked to admit by his sheer dark fury. There was more volatile emotion than she had ever thought he possessed emanating from him and lacing the atmosphere with brutal tension. Unfortunately, it wasn't how she would've wanted to discover that he was much more emotional in nature than he was prepared to show.

'*Sì*, an interview. While I'm busy hiring extra security to *protect* you, you're still feeding the fire to gain the attention you crave from your admirers!'

Brooke took a mental step back from the

toweringly tall, dark man raging over her and concentrated on the article. She was quick to recognise that stray comments she had made and medical info that should've been kept confidential had been cobbled together and leaked in the form of an interview that had been faked. 'I didn't give anyone an interview, Lorenzo. I did let one of the nurses take a photo of me and I'm sorry she gave it to the press, but I didn't exactly know who I was supposed to be then or that I shouldn't allow that,' she confided uncomfortably. 'Read it properly and you'll see I'm telling the truth. It's a *fake* interview. I wouldn't want people to know that I'm suffering from amnesia because that's embarrassing—'

'Unfortunately for you,' Lorenzo countered glacially, 'I already know that I can't trust a word you say because you're a gifted liar. You lie about the most ridiculous things and then shrug indifferently when the truth comes out. I've never been able to trust you!'

While Brooke had contrived to remain calm and in control while Lorenzo vented his wrath over a naïve mistake she had made, those words fell on her like hand grenades that exploded on contact with her shrinking body. In shock, she drew up her knees and hugged them. All her natural colour had gone into retreat while her tummy stirred sickly. She had told her husband lies and he had found her out in them? *She* was a liar? It dawned on her then that for the very *first* time Lorenzo was giving her what he deemed to believe was the absolute truth about herself, yet only raw anger had drawn that honesty from him. For just a few minutes he had forgotten to treat her like someone too delicate to handle reality.

All of a sudden, she was being forced to face the fact that, regardless of how hard she had tried to explain away her husband's cool attitude towards her, their relationship *did* have problems. Indeed, Lorenzo saw her as a liar he couldn't trust. Shaken and appalled by that revelation, she rocked back and forth where she sat, struggling to deal with that new sobering knowledge.

Lorenzo stared down at her and then he blinked and the explosive rage that had powered him, most ironically a rage that had never once seized him with Brooke before, vanished as though it had never been.

Stricken by what he had dumped on her in a temper, he came down on the side of the bed and hauled in a deep shuddering breath, cursing his lack of control and the damage he had inflicted. She looked so small, so lost, so unlike the woman he remembered, the woman he needed to *bury* and forget about because *that* version of Brooke might never return, he finally acknowledged.

'I'm sorry. I shouldn't have lost my temper,' Lorenzo conceded heavily and reached for her hand. 'When I saw that paper, a fuse just blew somewhere inside me *and*—'

'We're both living in a very stressful situation,' Brooke pointed out in a wobbly undertone. 'It's sure to be affecting you as well.'

Lorenzo didn't feel that he was in a stressful situation because naturally he was in possession of facts she had yet to learn. But he did feel guilty, horrendously guilty for shouting at her, condemning her and causing her distress. When her hand pulled away from his, rejecting that hold, he was disconcerted by that withdrawal.

'You don't need to pretend any longer, Lorenzo,' Brooke sighed in explanation.

'You've let the cat out of the bag. We don't have a good marriage, which actually explains *a lot*.'

Unprepared for that far-reaching conclusion being reached at such speed, Lorenzo hesitated only a moment before reaching across the bed and bundling her small resisting figure into his arms and settling her down across his long muscular thighs with an intimacy he had never dared to embrace before. 'No, it only explains that I have a terrible temper, which I usually manage to keep in check,' he breathed as he heard her swallow back the sobs making her tremble within his grasp. 'It doesn't mean anything.'

'But you said I was always telling lies and that you couldn't trust me!' Brooke sobbed outright.

Lorenzo was usually very fast at thinking on the back foot, as it were, but a quicksilver tongue somehow evaded him when he had Brooke struggling to hold back sobs in his arms. *He* had done that; *he* alone had distressed her to that extent. Yet she had borne every unsettling, scary development bravely from the outset of her recuperation. Even so, he had, and for the second time, reduced her to tears. He felt like a complete heel. When had he become so tough, bitter and selfish that he only went through the motions of giving her a roof over her head while at the same time utterly ignoring her presence in every other way? Of course, she had noticed that he wasn't behaving like a husband, of course she had become anxious about it.

'Did I lie about money?' Brooke whispered chokily. 'I mean, I can see by that wardrobe that I was kind of a bit…spendthrift.'

Lorenzo seized on that option with intense relief. He was rich enough to support a thousand spendthrift wives but rows over extravagance and lies concerning that extravagance were far less damaging to her self-image than the truth would be. 'Yes,' he confirmed, relieved to feel some of the jerking rigidity in her small frame drain away. 'Nothing I couldn't deal with, but you kept on doing it.'

'Well, I won't any more,' Brooke whispered shakily, the worst of her crushing anxiety draining away. 'I promise you, absolutely promise that I won't tell you any lies or spend too much money. There's no limit on those credit cards you gave me, is there?'

Lorenzo breathed in deep and slow. 'I don't think we need to worry about that now. You've only spent a couple of hundred pounds since you arrived,' he reminded her ruefully. 'Believe me, you can be a lot more spendthrift than that. I don't want you worrying about that either.'

'Maybe getting married to someone with money like you have sort of went to my head and I got carried away,' Brooke suggested thoughtfully.

Lorenzo registered the one salient fact that he should have shared with her sooner. 'No, you weren't penniless when I married you—your father left you a decent trust fund. He was an affluent wine importer and you were an only child.'

Brooke focused huge violet eyes on him as she flung her head back. 'I have money of my own?' she exclaimed incredulously.

'Yes, although we agreed when we married that I would take care of all the bills.'

But Brooke was still gripped by amazement that she had her own money. 'That really surprises me because I don't feel like

I've ever had money. I suppose that sounds weird to you when I obviously have, but everything like the staff here and the limousines and the grandeur makes me feel... overwhelmed,' she finally confided. 'I assumed it was because I hadn't had time yet to become accustomed to your lifestyle.'

'Your parents weren't rich, only comfortably off,' Lorenzo suggested, the feel of her body heat, the brush of her breasts against his shirtfront and her proximity combining to increase the hard arousal thrumming at his groin and remind him of just how long it had been since he had had sex. As gently as he could, he scooped her up, rose upright and laid her back down on the bed. 'You should rest. I upset you.'

Brooke sat up again. 'I'm fine now. The nurse that took that photo was called Lizzie and if you read the supposed interview, you can see it's just put-together stuff aside of the amnesia.'

Lorenzo lifted the paper he had slapped down in front of her and spread his free hand, long brown fingers flexing. 'My temper went off like a rocket. I didn't read it and I'll inform the clinic about the nurse.'

'I don't want her to get in trouble!' Brooke protested.

'She sold a photo of you and revealed confidential medical facts. The clinic needs to protect their patients,' Lorenzo murmured smoothly, still incensed by the condemnation he had immediately laid at his wife's door and the distress the episode had caused her.

The distress *he* had created by jumping to conclusions without proof and venting freely. He swore to himself that it would be the very last time he awarded blame to her on the basis of her past sins. He really hadn't thought through the extent of the responsibility he was taking on in bringing her back to what had once been her home. And now he was stuck fast, neither married nor divorced, his own life in limbo alongside hers…

And for how long could he tolerate that injustice?

Lorenzo returned to the bank. Brooke went out to the garden, which she loved, strolling along gravel paths, enjoying the sunlight and the flowers and greenery all around her. A little dog bounded out from below the trees and began to bark at her. Brooke laughed because it was a tiny little thing, a mop of tousled multi-shaded brown hair on four spindly legs.

'Now who do you belong to?' she asked, settling down on a bench when natural curiosity brought the dog closer. He jumped up against her legs, more than willing to invite attention. She petted him, lifted him and discovered that *he* was a girl and laughed again, letting her curl up on her lap and settle there.

The gardener nearby, engaged in freshening up a bed with new plants, glanced across the sunken garden at them in apparent surprise. When she moved on, the little dog followed at her heels and she said to the gardener. 'Who does the dog belong to?'

'Topsy's yours, Mrs Tassini,' he said without hesitation and she realised that her amnesia was no longer a secret, if it ever had been, in the household.

Only a slight flush on her cheeks, Brooke walked on before stooping to pet the little animal. Her dog had found the way back to her and she smiled, delighted to discover that she had a pet and that she liked animals. It was uplifting to learn that there had been a positive side to the self she no longer remembered because so far she only appeared to be finding out negative stuff, she conceded ruefully, thinking about the extravagance and the lies that had clearly damaged her marriage. At the same time though, it was better to be forewarned that there could be further obstacles ahead, she reflected ruefully. What else had she done that she would be ashamed to find out?

At least, Lorenzo had resisted the very human urge to just dump all her mistakes on her at once, she thought fondly. That had been generous of him in the circumstances. He was doing everything by the book and shielding her from unpleasant truths. How could she not love a man like that?

Brooke dressed for dinner that evening with greater care than usual. Finally, she surveyed her reflection in one of the several mirrors in the dressing room and something strange happened. For a timeless instant as she gazed into the mirror, she became dizzy and she saw another woman. No, it wasn't *another* woman, she realised with a spooked shiver of reaction, it was herself clad in a black jacket with her hair straight and wearing a different red dress. She had been sitting in the back of a limousine. She blinked rapidly and realised that she had *finally* remembered something from the past and she couldn't wait to tell Mr Selby about that promising little glimmer.

It wouldn't be worth mentioning it to Lorenzo though, would it? Just as she hadn't thought to mention that none of the ravishing shoes in the cabinets even fitted her any longer because evidently her feet had grown a little fatter and those shoes pinched like the devil. A tiny little flashback that only involved seeing herself and that showed her nothing important wasn't worth telling Lorenzo about. Even so, it was a promising start to a complete recovery.

Lorenzo was still upstairs when she arrived in the dining room and she walked out onto the terrace that overlooked the garden, wondering if it would be acceptable to suggest that they ate outside during the summer months because the evenings were so beautiful and she did love the fresh air. Careful in the high heels that she was still a little wobbly in and with Topsy in tow, because the little dog hadn't left her side all day, she descended the steps that led down to the garden and roved along a path that led into a shrubbery backed by natural woodland. Topsy went scampering ahead and then started barking so ferociously that she almost levitated off the ground.

'Topsy,' she began to say and then, before she could gather her breath, a man leapt out of nowhere in front of her and gave her such a fright that she screamed.

And screamed again, backing away in absolute terror, every natural instinct on high alert, her heart thundering in her ears with fear. The man threw up his hands in apparent disbelief and then two men appeared from behind him and pulled him away.

An arm snaked round her quaking figure from behind. 'Are you all right?' Lorenzo's very welcome and familiar voice enquired, and relief made her sag like a ragdoll in his arms. 'I was in the dining room when I heard you scream. I've never moved so fast in my life!'

'Who was he?' she prompted shakily. 'What did he want?'

'A paparazzo chancing his arm,' Lorenzo imparted. 'Didn't you notice his camera?'

'No… I thought… I thought he was a rapist or something,' she contrived to explain unevenly, her breath still see-sawing in and out of her raw throat. 'That's what I assumed. I didn't think about this being a garden and how unlikely that would be, which was stupid.'

Lorenzo's dark eyes glittered with wildly inappropriate appreciation of that explanation for Brooke's reaction to a member of the press and he made no comment, seeing for himself that she was still pale and trembling with fright. He closed an arm round her to direct her back indoors. 'You can blame me for this frightening experience as well,' he told her instead in an exasperated undertone. 'I was about to double our security before I saw that newspaper headline this morning and then I *forgot*.'

'You're allowed to overlook stuff occasionally,' Brooke told him, still struggling to get her breathing under control. 'Anyway, how can it be *your* fault when it's obvious that my love of attracting publicity caused all this nonsense?'

'It wasn't wrong for you to like attracting publicity,' Lorenzo countered levelly. 'That was your world. I shouldn't have given you the impression that it was a bad choice, because it wasn't for you.'

But it was a bad choice for anyone married to you, Brooke completed inside her head, for everything about Lorenzo implied that he was a very private man and the last man imaginable to enjoy that kind of exposure. Clearly, her past self hadn't much cared about that, and she had continued to relentlessly pursue her own goals. She was twenty-eight years old and could scarcely blame that decision on immaturity. She had put her media career first, *not* her marriage.

'Topsy!' she called, and the dog raced over to her, long silly ears flopping madly, tongue hanging. Without hesitation she scooped the little animal up and started telling it that it was a great little watchdog while Lorenzo looked on in disbelief.

Brooke didn't *like* animals, but some nameless admirer had gifted her the puppy when handbag dogs were in vogue. She had brought the dog home and abandoned it in the kitchen and, as far as he knew, had never looked at it again. Lorenzo decided it was time for him to have another chat with her psychiatrist and ask how it was possible that his wife could be displaying entirely new personality traits as well as different tastes. Brooke wasn't even eating salads any longer, never mind fussing about her diet. She no longer used the gym and barely touched alcohol aside of a glass of wine at dinner. The changes were piling up to the extent that he no longer knew what to expect from the wife he would once have sworn that he knew inside out.

'Would you like a drink after that... er rather unnerving encounter?' he asked calmly.

'No, thanks. But thanks for being there this morning and this evening to ground me,' Brooke murmured in a rush, staring up at him with a great burst of warmth rushing and spreading through her veins, because she was grateful, *so* ridiculously grateful that Lorenzo existed and that she was married to him. He was her rock in every storm.

'I wasn't there for you this morning in the way I should've been,' Lorenzo corrected with a sardonic twist of his beautiful shapely mouth, tensing as that warm look in her eyes somehow contrived to arrow straight down to his groin. 'I attacked you, misjudged you.'

Determined violet eyes connected with his. 'But I forgive you.'

'Too easily,' Lorenzo chided, trying to keep some distance between them while he was as hard as rock and throbbing with arousal.

Brooke realised that she was literally backing him into the wall and she laughed in surprise, wondering if Lorenzo was always so slow on the uptake, so business-like, so prone to saying and doing only the right thing that he couldn't even grasp when his wife was coming on to him! She lifted her hands and ran them up over his ribcage over the shirt below his tailored jacket, sensitive fingertips learning the lean mouth-watering musculature hidden beneath, and she stretched up and literally face-planted her mouth on his.

Two very masculine hands sank into her mane of ringlets and held her fast and she smiled against his parting lips, her mouth opening eagerly for the plunging urgency of his. It was everything she remembered from the clinic, a chemical explosion of sheer hunger and demand. Oh, yes, her husband *wanted* her all right, she savoured with pleasure, he only needed encouragement while she needed no encouragement whatsoever when keeping her hands off him was more of a challenge. Her body was coming alive with a host of sensations from the tightening of her nipples, to the swell of her breasts, to the aching hollowness that tugged at the heart of her.

There was a sound somewhere behind her and Lorenzo yanked her back from him as though he had been burned. Stevens was muttering an apology and Lorenzo assured him that dinner *right now* was fine.

Her face hot as hellfire, so hot she wanted to die for a split second, Brooke retreated to her designated dining chair and grasped her wine glass with new fervour. She couldn't look at Lorenzo, she absolutely couldn't look at him in that instant, she was so mortified by her own forward behaviour, but honestly, it was as if he were a magnet that pulled at her until she couldn't resist the charge any more. She was convinced that she had never felt desire so strongly before…and yet how could that be?

Lorenzo infuriated her then by acting as if nothing had happened. He asked her about her day and her enjoyment of the garden. Slowly, painfully, her equilibrium returned. It wasn't *his* fault that she wanted him to be the sort of guy who said to hell with dinner and carted her off to the nearest private spot to take advantage of her willingness... *was it?*

CHAPTER FIVE

IT WAS NOW or never, Brooke challenged herself, because on a deep inner level she was cringing about what she was about to do.

The many mirrors in her dressing room showed a slender figure garbed in a white satin and lace nightdress. Wearing it felt weird because Brooke was convinced that, at heart, she was a pyjama girl rather than the fashionable, sexier image she was sporting, but, going by the decorative lingerie collection in the dressing room, her past self had never given way to the weakness of putting comfort first. Pyjamas weren't sexy though and she *needed* sexy, needed it desperately, she acknowledged apprehensively, because in spite of reading the book she had found in the bedside cabinet on 'how to thrill your lover,' she *still* felt as if she didn't have a clue!

After all, suppose Lorenzo *rejected* her?

How would she ever rise above that humiliation? She breathed in deep. Her need to have a normal marriage, added to the desire she definitely felt for him, was motivating her and what was wrong with making a major effort? Why would he reject her when he kissed her as though his life depended on it? she asked herself, striving to bolster her flagging courage as she ranged closer to the connecting door between their bedrooms and reached for the handle. The blasted door was locked! She couldn't believe it, and so afraid was she of losing her nerve altogether that she stalked straight out of her bedroom and walked down the corridor to let herself into his room with a fast-beating heart.

She couldn't believe her luck when she heard the shower running in the en suite. In one frantic leap she made it into the bed and hit the lights on the wall to plunge the room into darkness. Maybe that was a little too cowardly, she reasoned with a grimace, because that amount of self-consciousness wasn't sexy either. Stretching up, she put the lights back on and surveyed his bedroom décor, which was much warmer and comfier in ambience than her own stark white bower of rest.

Brooke was still all of a quiver, like a real scaredy-cat. She shrank at the prospect of being confronted by Lorenzo's shock, surprise and, ultimately, his rebuff. But if he said no, he would have to explain why not, wouldn't he? And then another little piece of the mystery of their marriage would fall into place, so, at the cost of her dignity, she would find out more even if he did dismiss her.

Lorenzo was in a dark brooding mood as he stepped out of the shower and snatched at a towel to dry off his hair. It was a challenge for him to believe that sharing a roof with Brooke could wind him up like a clockwork toy with sheer lust. How had that happened? *When* had that happened? It was damned near three years since he had experienced that hunger and then Brooke had woken up after the accident and somehow that primal urge had come back with a vengeance, engulfing him without reason or logic. It infuriated him.

When Lorenzo strode naked out of the

bathroom and saw her lying in his bed, the last chain of restraint snapped inside him and set him free. Suddenly he had had it with self-discipline and had it with continually hearing his legal team's warnings in the back of his mind and all he could think about was that there were no cameras in his bedroom and he could do whatever the hell he liked with the woman he had married. Brooke was still his wife. He wanted her and *she* wanted *him*. If he kept it that simple, he didn't need to even think about anything else, and it *was* simple, basic sexual instinct and nothing more.

'I th-thought...' Brooke stammered, peering in awe at him over the top of the duvet, striving to grab up some bad-girl sass from somewhere down deep inside her, so deep she couldn't find it. She felt like a woman who had never been in a man's bed in her life and that was unsettling her more and increasing her nerves.

'Great minds think alike,' Lorenzo quoted, all smooth and dark in tone like the finest chocolate laced with that delicious accent of his.

And he smiled at her, he actually *smiled*,

and the charisma of that smile set her heart-beat racing and released butterflies in her tummy. In an abrupt movement, Brooke pushed back the duvet with valiant hands and sat up against the pillows, the worst of her nerves conquered by the suspicion that she could have looked as though she was hiding in his bed like a little kid. A deep heat assailed her face when she registered that he was naked, absolutely naked, all bronzed and hair-roughened and aroused naked, and her mouth ran dry.

'So,' she breathed shakily. 'You're not going to throw me out?'

Lorenzo tilted his tousled and damp dark head to one side and sent her a smoulder-ing appraisal from dark glittering eyes that speared her where she sat. 'You want me?'

Unnerved a bit by the change in his at-titude, Brooke nodded jerkily like a mari-onette.

'Say it,' Lorenzo commanded, needing to hear the words because he knew she didn't remember being with him before and that for her this was her first time with him.

'I want you,' Brooke practically whispered, so hard was it to get sufficient oxygen into her struggling lungs.

'*Dannazione*... No, I'm not going to throw you out,' Lorenzo told her thickly.

'I want us to have a normal marriage,' she muttered tightly.

'It's been a long time since we had normal,' Lorenzo admitted.

'But why *is* that?' she pressed.

'That's not something we want to get into at this moment,' Lorenzo growled, tossing aside the towel still clutched in one lean brown hand and climbing into the bed.

Brooke felt almost as if she couldn't breathe with Lorenzo that close, the heat of his body warming hers even before he touched her, and then his wide sensual mouth crashed down on hers and breathing began to seem a much overrated pursuit as every sense she possessed flew off on a wild and wonderful trail of discovery. The very scent of him, soap, designer cologne and clean male, overwhelmed her and the minty taste of him against her tongue was delicious. As for the actual feel of that long, lean, hot, heavy body pressing against hers, it invoked a delirious wriggle closer from her hips while she pushed her breasts against the hard wall of his chest.

Great minds think alike.

She loved that phrase, which suggested that he had been waiting for her. Maybe this had always been their way—she came to him—and the idea no longer bothered her because he was pushing the welcome mat out with irrefutable enthusiasm.

Think about what you're doing.

The words sounded somewhere in Lorenzo's brain like an alarm bell but he suppressed them fast. He was way past caring *how* Brooke had contrived to make him want her again. He was fed up with being sensible when she drew him now on a very primitive level that kept him awake at night, wondering, fantasising about a woman who only eighteen months earlier he could not wait to kick out of his life. He stressed too much about making mistakes, he told himself impatiently. For once he would just go with the flow and do what seemed entirely natural.

Without ceremony he stripped off the nightdress and her breath caught in her throat again as she looked up at him. He had such beautiful eyes, lustrous gold in the lower lighting and framed by dense black lashes that curled up at the ends. Breathless, she lay there entranced until his warm, sensual mouth sealed to hers and a great swoosh of heat rushed up through her as a large masculine hand curved round a plump breast, the thumb rubbing at the sensitive tip until she gasped. Instantaneously she wanted more and when he utilised his mouth instead to suck at the swollen bud, she marvelled that even amnesia could make her forget such distinct sensations.

The tug on her nipple set alight the burn between her thighs, the pulsing liquidity that turned her to mush. She pushed against him in helpless need and he laughed softly, even that sound surging through her like an added aphrodisiac. She ran her hands down his sleek, satiny back with new confidence, smoothing over a lean flank, mentally recalling the book that had specified 'firm, assured' as the most desirable touch and wondering how on earth she could've forgotten something so basic as how to make love to her husband. However, when she touched him, he froze, and she jerked her fingers away again in swift retreat from that daring.

'No…no, don't back off,' Lorenzo positively purred in her ear, returning her small fingers to their former destination and revelling in her enthusiasm. 'I *like* being touched.'

Confidence renewed, Brooke stroked her hand along that smooth velvety skin, fascination powering her in her exploration of all that made them different. But a little of her attention seemed to go a long way and, before she got very far, Lorenzo was spreading her across the mattress like a starfish and she was a little nervous of that position until he began to work his path down her splayed body employing both his mouth and his hands to investigate her curves. The warm damp feeling at her core increased exponentially, leaving her craving his touch to an extent that was almost unbearable to her straining body.

'You've been driving me crazy with hunger for weeks,' Lorenzo growled, kissing a deeply intimate trail up her inner thigh, reducing her to uneasy little twists and jerks of a curious but self-conscious nature.

'Have I?' she pressed, half an octave

higher, the words strangling in her throat as he ran his tongue over her most sensitive area, and her hands snapped into fists of restraint because she wanted to sink her fingers into that tousled dark hair of his.

'Every time I look at you, I want you,' Lorenzo grated, stringing a line of kisses across her quivering belly.

'Doesn't show!' she gasped, ridiculously grateful that she had gone leaping into his bed and weak with relief because Lorenzo didn't show things, didn't usually talk like this to her. Evidently, he needed a certain level of intimacy to get comfortable enough to share such truths.

He dallied between her thighs, making moves that drove her to the outer edge of hunger, and every nerve ending was screaming for release and then it happened, in a magical great whoosh that exploded through her being like a shooting star, a drowning absolute pleasure that drenched every limb and left her with a sense of shock that anything could feel that physically good.

That achieved, Lorenzo shifted over her with an intense look of hunger in his dark glittering eyes and it made her feel like a million dollars and as if every path in her life were paved with solid gold. Her heart clenched because the more she found out about him, the more she wanted him, and it was a heady moment that made her eyes prickle with tears, making her blink and turn her head away as his hands slid beneath her hips to tilt her up to him.

And in the next moment, he surged into her ready body, although her body didn't react as though it had been ready for that masculine invasion. It hurt, it hurt *a lot* and almost startled Brooke into crying out, but she mercifully managed to hold onto the cry that almost parted her lips because she was sure that that would have spoilt everything. He would have blamed himself for causing her pain when surely the only reason she had suffered pain lay in the reality that it had been well over a year since she had had sex. And that wasn't anybody's fault, she conceded ruefully.

It was a relief when the discomfort ebbed entirely, and she was able to lose herself again in the intimacy. Her heart began to pound with every lithe thrust of his body over and inside hers, excitement climbing, breathlessness ensured as she wrapped her legs round his lean hips and savoured the sweet throbbing pleasure engulfing her. The hunger came back, urging her body to shift up to his, and little sounds escaped her without her true awareness since it was a passion beyond anything she thought she could ever have felt. The excitement was overwhelming, all-consuming and she wanted more and more until she rose against him on a feverish wave of wild pleasure and another orgasm took her in a rush of high-wire energy.

'Wow,' she whispered in the aftermath, flaking out back against the pillows, limp and drained but secretly triumphant as well because she had achieved exactly what she had set out to do.

'Incredible,' Lorenzo commented, collapsing down beside her out of breath while he dimly wondered how sex could possibly be so different with her that even her behaviour had changed, and he felt as though he was with a different woman. Yes, he was definitely going to see Mr Selby for the question and answer session that he badly needed. Although he doubted if he would mention their new intimacy because that was private…wasn't it? Was *anything* between them private now? he asked himself in disbelief at the concept.

'I'm not on the pill,' Brooke murmured with a sudden stab of anxiety, for she suspected that the very last thing they dared risk in a marriage that appeared to need rebuilding would be a child. 'Did you—?'

'You have an IUD,' Lorenzo assured her while it dawned on him that, even so, he should have taken precautions because she had been with other men. On the other hand, while in medical care she had been saturated with every antibiotic known to man.

His contraceptive omission, however, was another concern that he was in no mood to deal with. It was, after all, a reminder of the true state of play between them and he suppressed the thought of it because if he thought about it too much, it would drive him crazy. The entire situation was *already* driving him crazy, he acknowledged as he questioned the secrecy he had been urged to embrace for her benefit.

But *was* it for her benefit?

Would she have slept with him were she herself?

And without warning, Lorenzo was snatched back into a black and white world with no forgiving shades of grey again. Brooke had hated him when he demanded a divorce and hadn't once spoken a civil word to him during their time apart when he had been forced out of his own house by her infidelity into a city apartment he had hated.

'We shouldn't have done this!' Lorenzo exclaimed with startling abruptness, feeling as though he had taken unfair advantage of her even though *she* was the one who had issued the invitation. 'You're not yourself… you don't know what you're doing.'

Brooke was galvanised out of her comfortable relaxation while thinking how weird it was that he had known she was on birth control when she did not. Even so, it was something she could live with until he said what he did, which filled her with a sensation very close to panic because she did not want him regretting what they had just shared. 'No, *no*, it's not like that!' she argued fervently.

'It is exactly like that,' Lorenzo contradicted gravely. 'I don't *like* that it feels like that but facts are facts.'

'No! You're not allowed to think like that now!' Brooke told him almost fiercely as she scrambled up and literally perched on top of him like a naked nymph, he reasoned in wonderment as arousal kicked in again for him with shocking immediacy.

'Why not?' Lorenzo breathed almost bitterly. 'I took advantage of you.'

'No, you didn't!' Brooke protested, leaning over him, her hands planted either side of his head on the pillows, the twin peaks of her luscious breasts brushing his chest. 'I got into *your* bed, for goodness' sake! I wanted you and we had a great time and that's all there is to it!'

Lorenzo blinked at that hail of keen protest and gazed up into vivid violet eyes and a flawless heart-shaped face surrounded by a tangle of platinum curls. His hands went up before he even knew it himself and he tasted her pouting pink lips like a man starving for that particular flavour. Need surged through him stronger than ever, a bone-deep driving need that threatened to unnerve him.

'I think I'm falling in love with you again, Lorenzo,' Brooke declared.

Lorenzo froze as though she had paralysed him. It was an interesting response from a husband in receipt of such a proclamation, she acknowledged unhappily.

'You can't love me...you don't know me,' he told her levelly.

'I beg to differ. It's almost three months since I came out of that coma and throughout that time you have been my biggest and best support team,' Brooke countered strongly. 'I have got to know you. I have got to see how you put me and my needs first *every time*. I have been here while you lived through a profoundly challenging situation with me and still took nothing for yourself. So please don't tell me that I *can't* love you because I don't know you. I do know what I've seen and how it makes me feel. I'm *definitely* falling for you.'

Lorenzo took a deep breath and parted his lips as if he was about to say something. But then he closed his mouth again and tugged her back down to him. 'Whatever,' he breathed, urgently conscious of her curvy body moving over his groin. 'I still want you.'

'Nothing wrong with that,' Brooke assured him, her colour rising headily as he gazed up at her full of blatant sexual intent.

'*Dio...cara mia,*' Lorenzo ground out, all self-discipline beaten down, even that affectionate label extracted from him by the encouraging feel of her in his arms. 'So, I'm free to live out my every fantasy, then?'

'Pretty much,' she whispered, barely recognising herself from the shy, uncertain woman she had been a mere hour earlier.

'I have quite an appetite built up,' he warned her thickly.

'It seems I have too,' Brooke whispered, recognising the hot tight sensation in her pelvis for the desire that it was this time around and ever so slightly proud of herself for no longer feeling either so ignorant or insecure about her own body. Lorenzo wanted her; indeed he had said that every time he looked at her, he wanted her. Why hadn't she had the perception to see that for herself in the man she had married? Why was her brain so dense where he was concerned? Why wasn't there even a glimmer of natural insight?

Stashing away her increasing frustration with her inability to remember what she needed to remember, Brooke fell into Lorenzo's blazingly sexual kiss, every concern about her ability to be sexy laid to rest. She was enough for *him* and really, at that moment, that was all that mattered to her or seemed the least bit important. He settled her down over him and raised her hips and, seconds later, she realised that it was all beginning again as he eased into her slow and sure, controlling her every movement in an innately dominant way while touching her in a way that sent her flying off the planet again within minutes. Exhausted then, she rested her head down on a smooth brown muscular shoulder and smiled dizzily.

Lorenzo surveyed his wife over breakfast with a faintly dazed light new to his shrewd dark gaze. There she was, curled up in a chair being all affectionate, playful and teasing while munching on toast and feeding Topsy pieces of crust. Brooke didn't eat carbohydrates; Brooke treated carbs like poison. He had never known her to be affectionate or playful either, even before he had married her. Within the hour, he was meeting with her psychiatrist in search of advice.

'Yes, I think it's perfectly possible that she could be a *very* different person without that celebrity frame of reference that was once so crucial to her self-image,' the older man declared with confidence. 'There are documented examples of cases of this nature but I'm afraid I can't tell you how to proceed. That is *your* decision, but I suspect it may soon be time to tell her that you were pursuing a divorce before the accident.'

Lorenzo mulled that challenging suggestion over on the way to the Tassini Bank for a board meeting and he grimaced. Last night they had had sex. Today he admits they're in the midst of a divorce? He breathed in slow and deep and groaned. That wouldn't work. He would sense the right moment to tell her when it arrived, he reasoned, recognising that he didn't want to rock the boat or cause her distress. It was still his role to be supportive, *not* destructive.

On the other hand, he was equally aware that he would never consider *staying* married to Brooke—he could not pardon either her lies or her infidelity. And that acknowledgement plunged him straight back into the same, 'damned if he did' and 'damned if he didn't' scenario...

Quite unaware of Lorenzo's thorny dilemma, Brooke was getting dressed to go out, which was something of a challenge given the glitzy nature of the contents of her dressing room. She knew that she didn't have to wear black to offer condolences, but it seemed a matter of respect for her to wear something other than a party outfit. She chose a navy pencil skirt and a silk striped top but she couldn't get the skirt to zip up and had to take it off again and accept with a wince that she had evidently put on weight. A pair of loose dark palazzo pants replaced the skirt. As she left the house for the first time since her arrival, she felt stronger and braver and relieved that she had finally got the gumption to do what she felt she had to do to lay her accident to rest in her own mind.

Lorenzo's PA at the bank had sounded surprised when Brooke phoned her but had been happy to pass on the address and the details she knew about the driver and the passenger who had died in the crash.

Brooke bent her head out of view when she saw the cluster of paparazzi at the foot of the drive. Lorenzo's disdain for their interest in his wife had been palpable and she marvelled that she had married a man who cherished his privacy when her own interests had clearly pushed her in a very different direction.

The driver's mother was delighted with her gift of flowers and pleased to have the chance to talk about her late son. She referred several times to the substantial tips that Brooke had regularly given her son and Brooke smiled, relieved to hear that she had been generous. Visiting Milly Taylor's grave, however, put her in a more sombre mood. Although enquiries had been made, only the young woman's former employer had claimed to know her, and that café would be Brooke's final destination.

The gravestone was simple. Brooke set down her floral offering and sighed, wondering if the woman had been a friend. It would make sense that she had had *one* friend, wouldn't it? But would she have made friends with someone from such a very different background? What would they have had in common?

The café was within walking distance of the cemetery and she had asked her driver to pick her up in half an hour. On the way there she passed a newsstand on the pavement and something caught her eye on a front page. She paused to lift the magazine. It was her face and across it was splashed: *Divorce or Reconciliation?*

'You need to buy it to read it,' the vendor told her irritably and she dug into her purse for the cash, her face heating.

She stood in the street reading the article inside and shock went crashing through her in wave after wave. Her tummy succumbed to a queasy lurch and she felt dizzy. Suddenly everything she had believed she knew about Lorenzo was being turned on its head! And equally, everything she had believed she knew about herself was being torn to shreds. Rumours of affairs? Yes, she had seen those photos of her in nightclubs with other men, but she had assumed those men were work contacts or social connections, had never dreamt *that*…?

And Lorenzo had a business trip to Italy,

for which he was leaving that very evening, and he would be away for a week. If she wanted the chance to speak to him, she couldn't afford to wait, no, she needed to see him immediately…

CHAPTER SIX

'YOUR WIFE'S HERE to see you,' Lorenzo was informed an hour later at the bank.

Taken aback by that unexpected announcement, because Brooke had never once in all the time he had known her come to see him at the bank, Lorenzo rose from behind his desk.

Brooke entered and the instant he saw her face he knew that something was badly wrong. Her eyes had a sort of glazed look and she was very pale, her stance as she paused uncertainly halfway towards him stiff and unnatural.

'What's wrong?' he asked quietly. 'Although possibly I should be asking you what's right. This *is* the first time you've emerged from the house since you left the clinic.'

'I shouldn't have come here...er...where

you work,' Brooke muttered in belated appreciation of what she had done in her distraught frame of mind. 'I should've waited until you came home, so I'm going to just do that and we can talk before you leave for the airport.'

Lorenzo hauled out a chair from the wall before she could leave again. 'No, sit down. I can see that you're troubled about something. Tea? Coffee?'

'A coffee would be good,' she conceded flatly, hoping the caffeine would cut a path through the tangled turmoil of her emotions and miraculously settle her down at a moment when she felt as though the floor beneath her feet had fallen away.

She *was* too dependent on Lorenzo, she acknowledged with a sinking heart. Lorenzo was irreversibly stitched into everything she had thought and done and worried about since she had first wakened from the coma. Since awakening, she had built an entire life around him, and the idea that their marriage was simply a cruel mirage cut her off at the knees and left her drowning in a sea of insecurity and regrets.

The coffee arrived in record time and she

was relieved to have something to occupy her hands as she cradled the bone-china cup and marvelled that it was a cup instead of a beaker. That random thought brought a wry smile to her lips. In truth, she recognised, she was eager to think about anything other than the giant chasm that had opened up beneath her feet.

'I went to see Paul Jennings's mother this morning,' she revealed as an opening.

Lorenzo leant back fluidly against the side of his desk, embracing informality for her benefit while both his exquisitely tailored dark suit and her surroundings screamed huge influential office and very powerful occupant. He was gorgeous, she conceded rather numbly, and it was hardly surprising that she had become attached to the idea that he was *hers*. Any woman in her circumstances would've done the same thing, she told herself bracingly. Not only was he gorgeous and sexy and terrific in bed, he had been a rock for her through every step of her recovery process. Whatever the truth of their marriage was, she still owed him gratitude for his generosity.

'Yes, my PA mentioned your plans. I

thought it was great that you were finally emerging from the house,' Lorenzo commented. 'So, what went wrong?'

'Oh…nothing went wrong,' Brooke assured him tautly. 'I bought a magazine because I saw my face on the cover.'

'Dio...' Lorenzo bit out, tensing. 'I should've foreseen that you might do something like that.'

Quite deliberately, Brooke lifted her chin, her violet eyes clear and level, giving no hint of the turmoil inside her. 'You can't protect me from everything, Lorenzo…and you shouldn't be *trying* to protect me from the truth,' she told him tightly. 'If it's true that we were getting divorced before the accident, you should've told me weeks ago.'

Lorenzo shifted a lean brown hand in a sudden imperious movement that sought to silence her as he took a step forward.

'Of course, I know *why* you didn't tell me because someone like Mr Selby or some other clever doctor warned you that it might be too much for my battered little brain to handle,' Brooke framed steadily, ignoring his gesture. 'But I disagree with that kind of over-protective attitude because I'm back in the real world now and I *have* to adjust to it, no matter how tough or destabilising it is. I'm not a child.'

Lorenzo surveyed her, feeling strangely appreciative of her control and dignity in a very taxing situation, two responses that he had least expected from her. Brooke had always been more about hysterics and ranting and blaming everybody but herself when anything went wrong. He breathed in deep and accepted the inevitable. The truth was out and he couldn't deny it. 'We *were* pursuing a divorce at the time of the crash,' he admitted levelly.

'Why?' Brooke asked baldly.

Lorenzo studied her. She looked tiny in that chair and she was as white as a sheet. How was he supposed to tell the woman that she now was that she had played away with multiple men, indeed any man who suggested that he could advance her goal of breaking into the screen industry? Lorenzo had never had the slightest difficulty in delivering bad news. Indeed, it was integral to his role as a banker, but when it came to shattering the woman seated before him, he just couldn't drop the ugly truth on her at that moment. The divorce would've been a big enough blow to a woman who had told him that she thought she might love him only the night before. Never mind that that professed love was simply an assumption brought on by her amnesia. She was still being very brave and he admired that, and bad news was never *quite* as bad if it emerged piece by piece over a lengthier period of time, he told himself grimly.

'We were ill-suited, different goals, different outlook on life,' Lorenzo responded. 'I wanted children but you didn't. I wanted a home. You only wanted an impressive backdrop for your photos. Divorce was inevitable.'

Brooke nodded valiantly. 'And...er...the men, the affairs?'

'Rumours,' Lorenzo asserted valiantly. 'But I didn't enjoy the rumours.'

Brooke bent her head but breathed a little easier at that release from her biggest fear: that she was capable of that kind of betrayal and of cheating on him. 'Of course not,' she agreed flatly. 'Even without my memory, I can see that the woman I was and the man you are weren't a good match.'

Lorenzo had gone very quiet. He was thinking hard and fast, wondering whether to take her straight to that penthouse apartment he had bought her to cement their separation back into place. In rapid succession he pictured her there alone and potentially lost and he recoiled from that image while questioning his own sanity.

'And I really shouldn't be living in your home any more,' Brooke completed quietly, raising the point she knew she had to raise to set him free from feeling responsible for her.

Lorenzo's black lashes dropped down over his glittering eyes and every muscle in his lean, powerful frame jerked rigid. He *couldn't* let her go, at least, *not just yet*, he reasoned fiercely. She wasn't fit to be abandoned to sink or swim and that might not strictly be his business any more, but he still *felt* as though it were. Right now, a separation would be premature.

'I have a better solution,' he heard himself say before he had even quite thought through what he was about to say, a divergence from habit that shook him even as he spoke. 'I suggest you accompany me to Italy this evening.'

'To Italy?' Brooke gasped as if she had never heard of the country before, so disconcerted was she by that proposal at that particular moment.

'Yes, it would be good for you to escape the paparazzi and the publicity and enjoy some breathing space. You're a UK celebrity, pretty much unknown—' he selected that last word tactfully '—in Italy. We'll be left alone, free of this constant media speculation. A break is what we need.'

Brooke lifted her head, her heart, which had slowed to a dulled thud, suddenly picking up speed again. 'We?' she queried in a near croak.

'We,' Lorenzo stressed with vigour, some of his tension ebbing now that he could see a provisional way forward out of the current chaos.

'But we're getting a divorce,' Brooke reminded him shakily.

'The divorce has been on hold since the day of the crash. A few more weeks aren't going to make much difference at this point,' Lorenzo informed her with assurance. 'We can separate or divorce at any time. Let's not allow past decisions to control us in a different situation. Let's be patient a little while longer and see how things progress. Your memory may yet return.'

Brooke was plunged deep into shock all over again, the price of having been thrown from one extreme to yet another. She had come to his office to confront him with her heart being squeezed in a steel fist of pain. She had believed that their marriage was an empty charade already all but over and that it was her duty to finally set Lorenzo free, even though she loved him. She remained absolutely convinced that, even though she had made a mess of their marriage, she *still* loved him.

But to her astonishment, Lorenzo was reacting in an utterly unexpected way by offering her a second chance at their marriage. Wasn't that what he meant? For goodness' sake, what else *could* he mean? He didn't want to immediately reclaim his freedom as she had assumed. He was willing to wait…he was willing to continue living with her as her husband. A shaken, shuddering breath forced its passage up through her constrained lungs because relief was filling her almost to overflowing, liberating all the emotions that she had been fighting to suppress since she read about their divorce proceedings in that awful gossipy magazine. Her eyes stung horribly and flooded. She blinked rapidly, warding off the tears and hastily sipping at her cooling coffee.

Lorenzo reached down and rescued the shaking cup and saucer to set it aside, and scooped her up into his arms. It wasn't pity driving him, he told himself with ferocious certainty, it was a crazy, impossible mix of lust, responsibility, sympathy and fascination with the woman she now was. He was taking her to Italy with him. It was a done deal.

'I'm sorry,' she briefly sobbed against his shoulder before she got a grip on herself again and glanced up at him with a grimace of apology. 'It was the shock. I was *expecting*—'

'Keep it simple, like me,' Lorenzo urged. 'I'm practical and calculating and very typical of the male sex. I'm expecting you in my bed at night.'

An indelicate little snort of laughter escaped Brooke then, drying up the tears at source. 'Is that so?' she mumbled, a sudden shard of happiness piercing her.

'You haven't even asked me yet what *I* did wrong in our marriage,' he reproved. 'The mistakes weren't all on *your* side. I worked long hours, left you alone too much and only took you to boring dinner parties where everyone was talking about finance. You weren't happy with me either.'

'We'll see how Italy goes,' Brooke murmured softly. 'As you said, we can choose to part at any time, so neither of us need to feel trapped.'

'You're feeling trapped?' Lorenzo demanded without warning, an arctic light gleaming in his beautiful dark eyes.

'No…' Brooke toyed with a button on his jacket, striving not to flatter him with too much enthusiasm. 'I don't feel trapped at all. Maybe I've grown up a bit from the person I was before the crash. Obviously I've changed. I don't seem to want people with cameras chasing me. I seem to have lost what seems to have been an overriding interest in fashion and clothes…gosh, I'm going to be forced out shopping if you're taking me travelling. A lot of the clothes, and particularly the shoes, don't fit me now,' she confided ruefully.

'I'll organise someone to come to the house this afternoon and kit you out. I'll postpone the flight until early tomorrow morning,' Lorenzo informed her arrogantly. 'But that means I'll have to work late tonight... OK?'

'OK,' she agreed breathlessly.

Lorenzo stared down at her heart-shaped face while a *what-the-hell-am-I-doing?* question raced over and over through his brain. He concentrated instead on that luscious pink mouth and the ever-present throb at his groin and bent his head to taste those succulent lips.

Brooke fell into that kiss like honey melting on a grill. Her insides turned liquid and burned. It happened every time he kissed her, a shooting, thrilling internal heat that washed through her like a dangerous drug, lighting up every part of her body. She wanted to cling, but she wouldn't let herself, stepping back with a control that she was proud to maintain after her earlier emotionalism.

She reddened as she connected with his

brilliant dark eyes, which packed such a passionate punch. Maybe this very hunger was what had first brought them together and kept them together even when their relationship didn't work in other ways. Sadly, it was a sobering thought to accept that sexual attraction might have been the most they had ever had as a couple and all she had left to build on.

Obviously, naturally, she wanted more, she reflected ruefully. She wanted him to *stop* feeling as responsible for her as a man might feel about a helpless child. She wanted him to see and accept that she no longer needed to be handled with kid gloves, that she was an adult and able to cope with her own life, even if it did mean losing him in the process. And possibly that was what it *would* mean, she conceded unhappily, bearing in mind that their marriage had apparently been rocky from the start.

Yet where had the ambition-driven woman she had been gone? Where had all the knowledge she must have accumulated from the fashion world gone? Why didn't she care now about what style was 'in' and what was 'out'? Why was she most comfortable in a pair of ordinary jeans? Where now was the brash confidence that had fairly blazed out of the magazine cuttings in her press scrapbooks? Those were questions that only time, or the recovery of her memories, would answer. But facing up to more challenging situations alone would probably strengthen her and do her good, she told herself fiercely. She resolved to make that visit to the café to ask about Milly Taylor on the drive home. Perhaps that would help her work out what the connection had been between two ostensibly very different women.

The café was also a bakery and Brooke waited patiently until the queue of customers had gone and the older woman behind the counter looked at her for the first time. The woman's eyes rounded, and she paled, stepping back as though she had had a fright.

'*Milly?*' she exclaimed shakily, her hand flying up to her mouth in a gesture of confusion as she stared at the younger woman. 'No, no… I can *see* you're not Milly, but just for a moment there, the resemblance gave me such a shock!'

Brooke's brow pleated as she asked the

woman if they could have a chat. 'I'm Brooke Tassini. Milly died in the crash that I was injured in. You seem to think I resemble her... I've lost my memory,' she explained with a wince. 'I'm still trying to work out who Milly was to me.'

'Brooke? I'm Marge,' the middle-aged woman said comfortably as she moved out from behind the counter. 'When I get a better look at you, the resemblance isn't as striking as I first thought it was. But Milly had the same long curly hair and the same colour of eyes. Look, come and see the photo of her.'

Brooke crossed the café to scrutinise the small staff group photo on the wall, but it wasn't a very clear picture and she peered at the smiling image with a frown because she could see the extraordinary similarity of their features and colouring. 'When she was working here, did she ever mention me? I'm wondering now if she could be some distant relation, a cousin or something?'

'Milly didn't ever mention you,' Marge told her apologetically. 'She was a quiet girl. To be honest, I don't think she *had* much of a life outside work and she only worked here for a couple of months. I got the impression that she had moved around quite a bit, but I was still surprised that morning when she chucked her job in, because she had seemed content here. She said she had to quit because she had a family crisis.' Marge made a face. 'She seemed to forget that according to what she had once told me, she didn't *have* a family.'

'Oh…' Brooke breathed, acknowledging that she was no further on in her need to know who her companion had been and why they had been in the limousine together. The resemblance, though, that was a new fact, something that hadn't come out before, possibly because Marge wasn't in the right age group even to know who Brooke Tassini was or what she looked like, she reasoned while thanking the woman for her time.

As she walked to the door to leave, a startling image shot through her brain and for a split second it froze her in her tracks. In the flashback a man was standing over her where she sat in the café and shouting drunkenly at her while Marge flung the door wide to persuade him to leave. Brooke tried to hang onto that snapshot back in time, frantic to see more, know *more*. But nothing else came to her and embarrassment at the time she had already taken out of Marge's working day—Marge, who was already serving a new queue of customers at the counter—pushed her back out onto the street again in a daze.

Why did she never remember anything useful? she asked herself in frustration. Obviously she had visited the café at some point, presumably to see Milly, and Marge hadn't remembered her, which wasn't that surprising in a busy enterprise. What did still nag at Brooke, though, was the resemblance that Marge had remarked on and she had seen for herself. That was a rather strange coincidence, wasn't it? But how could it relate in any way to why that woman had been with her in the car?

CHAPTER SEVEN

BROOKE WAS RELAXED and calm on the drive from the airport in Florence.

Even the crack of dawn flight had failed to irritate her because the change of scene was a relief and an escape from her repetitive and anxious thoughts. Those exact same thoughts had threatened to send her out in search of more gossipy magazines that would enable her to find out additional stuff about her marriage. Aware of that temptation and the futility of such an exercise, when she already knew as much as she needed to know for the present, she had made herself concentrate instead on the selection of a capsule wardrobe with the stylist, who had arrived at Madrigal Court the previous afternoon. It had been a disappointment, though, that Lorenzo had come home so late that he had evidently chosen to sleep in his own room.

The crisp white and blue sundress she wore was comfortable in the heat of an Italian summer. It was neither edgy nor trendy but it was elegant and flattering, skimming nicely over those curvy parts of her that she was beginning to suspect were a little *too* curvy. Was a tendency to gain why she had once watched her diet with such zeal? But she had been too thin when she emerged from the coma and was now content to be a healthy weight, she reasoned. In any case, Lorenzo had been with her when she was flawless in figure and physically perfect and, clearly, it had done nothing to save their marriage. Now she had scars and more curves and neither seemed to bother him, although, to be fair, the scarring was minimal, thanks to the expert cosmetic surgery she had received, she acknowledged gratefully.

'Have I ever been to this house of yours before?' she asked Lorenzo.

'No. I tried to bring you here a couple of times, but it never fitted your schedule.

There was always some event, some opening or fashion show that you couldn't miss.'

'Did you grow up in this house?' she prompted with curiosity.

Lorenzo surprised her by laughing, amusement gleaming in his lustrous dark golden eyes. 'No. I bought and renovated it. Sometimes, I forget how little you know about me now. I grew up in a splendid Venetian palazzo on the Grand Canal with my father.'

'No mother around?' she pressed in surprise.

'No, sadly she died bringing me into the world. She had a weak heart,' Lorenzo volunteered. 'And I don't think my father ever forgave me for being the cause of her death. He told me more than once that she was the only woman he had ever loved and that I had taken her from him.'

'But that's so unjust. I mean—'

'Do you think I don't know that?' Lorenzo sent her a wryly amused glance at her bias in his defence. 'He was a self-centred man. My mother wanted a baby and took the risk of getting pregnant against doctor's orders and I got the blame for it. I believe my father could have adjusted quite happily to *not* having a son and heir. Maybe a daughter would've brought out a softer side to him... who knows? He died last year, and we never had a close relationship.'

'That's so sad, such a waste.' Brooke sighed regretfully. 'I wish my parents had lived long enough for you to meet them and then you could have told me something about them.'

'Being without family never seemed to bother you. I think that it was natural for you to be a loner.'

'Is that why you think I didn't want children?' she asked abruptly.

Lorenzo expelled his breath in a measured hiss. 'No, you had multiple reasons for that. The effect on your body, the risk to your potential career, the responsibilities that would eat into your ability to come and go as you pleased.'

Brooke nodded, getting the message that in the past she had *definitely* not wanted a child. Evidently, her career had meant everything to her and that tough decision surprised her because she had found herself watching young children visiting their relatives in the clinic and had easily and quickly warmed to their presence. But Lorenzo had to know the woman he had married best, particularly now that he was no longer glossing over the more sensitive subjects simply to keep her in the dark and supposedly protect her from herself. But how on earth was anyone to tell her how to cope with a self that she, increasingly, didn't like very much?

'Did I tell you that I didn't want a family before we got married?' she pressed.

'No,' Lorenzo framed succinctly. 'Knowing *that* I wouldn't have married you but, to be fair, you didn't lie about it either. Later, I realised that you had merely avoided saying anything that would've committed you.'

Brooke still saw that as sly, just as he had once labelled her, but she said nothing because the picture of their marriage she was getting was still better than the blank she had had before, even if the more she learned, the more she suspected that saving such a troubled relationship could be a steeper challenge than even she had imagined.

'Why are we even talking about this?' Lorenzo demanded with wry amusement. 'The last complication we need now is a child.'

'Yes,' she agreed a little stiffly because it was true: they had quite enough on their plate with her amnesia. 'So, what happened to the Venetian palazzo you grew up in? Or didn't you inherit it?'

'I did inherit. I converted it into an exclusive boutique hotel. I had no personal attachment to the place. My childhood memories aren't warm or fluffy,' he admitted.

'I wonder if mine are,' she murmured ruefully.

'I should think so. The way you told it, you were an adored only child.' Lorenzo closed a hand over her restive hands where they were twisting together on her lap. 'Stop fretting about what you don't know and can't help.'

'I've had a couple of flashbacks!' she heard herself admit rather abruptly. 'Mr Selby thinks that's very hopeful.'

Lorenzo frowned in disconcertion, annoyed that she hadn't told him first. 'What did you remember?'

'Only an image of me seated in a limo and one of me in that café where Milly Taylor worked and where I must have gone to meet her. Not very helpful or interesting,' she remarked with a sigh.

'But promising,' Lorenzo commented, wondering why he didn't feel more excited over the prospect of her reclaiming her memory and, consequently, her life. Was it possible that after so many months he had reached some stage of compassion fatigue and disappointed hopes where he was simply guilty of secretly wishing that his life would return to normal?

Dannazione, why didn't he just admit the truth to himself? This current version of Brooke was his unparalleled favourite. He was in no hurry to reclaim the original version. As she was now, she was likeable, desirable and surprisingly appealing. Naturally he preferred her this way, he conceded with gritty inner honesty, no great mystery there. Only a masochist would have craved the old Brooke. What was wrong with being truthful about that? The woman he was with now was neither the woman he had married nor the woman he had been divorcing.

Brooke peered out of the windows as the limo drove up a steep twisting lane hedged in by dense trees and her eyes widened with appreciation as the lane opened out to frame the rambling farmhouse that sat on top of a gentle hill, presiding, she suspected, over a spectacular view of the Tuscan countryside. 'It's a beautiful site,' she remarked.

'It's remote,' Lorenzo warned her as he climbed out of the car. 'You may find it quite isolated here while I'm away on business.'

'I think I'll be fine,' Brooke declared, waiting for the driver to open the car and bring Topsy's travelling carrier out. She bent down to release the little animal, accepting the frantic affection coming her way with a wide grin. 'I can go for walks with Topsy, sit out and read, maybe even do a little exploring.'

'I'm not planning to work *every* day,' Lorenzo told her with a sudden flashing smile. 'I don't want you going too far on your own, so save the exploration until I'm here and it will be much more comfortable for you.'

Topsy bouncing at her heels, Brooke walked into the house, violet eyes sparkling with pleasure at everything she saw. Her hand stretched out to brush the weathered pale sun-warmed stone of the house as if she couldn't resist its appeal. 'I love old things,' she told him cheerfully.

Lorenzo stoically resisted the urge to contradict her with his superior knowledge of her tastes. 'She's discovering herself again,' the psychiatrist had told him. 'Give her that freedom.'

'When did you buy this place?' she asked.

'Long before I met you. I wanted a home base in Italy, and I assumed I would use it for holidays but, to be frank, I've hardly been here since the renovation project was completed.'

Brooke gave his shoulder a playful mock punch. 'Because you work too hard,' she pointed out, gazing around the rustic hallway and caressing the smooth bannister of the old wooden staircase that led up to the next floor.

'You used a designer, didn't you?' she guessed, moving from doorway to doorway to study the pale drapes and the subtle palate of colours employed to provide a charming and tranquil backdrop to antique rustic furniture and comfortable contemporary sofas.

Lorenzo laughed, his lean dark features extraordinarily handsome in that moment as he stood in the sunshine flooding through the open front door. 'How did you guess?' he mocked.

'Whoever you used was really good,' Brooke was saying appreciatively when a sparely built older man appeared in the hallway and greeted them in a flood of Italian.

'This is Jacopo. He and his wife, Sofia, look after us here,' Lorenzo informed her, closing a hand round hers to urge her towards the stairs. 'When would you like lunch?'

'Midday? After our early start, I'm quite hungry.' She shot an uncertain glance up at his lean dark face, ensnared by vibrant and lustrous black-lashed golden eyes that left her breathless.

Lorenzo informed Jacopo and led her upstairs. 'Sofia likes a schedule to work to. She's a great cook.'

'Did I ever cook for you?' Brooke enquired.

'Never.'

Her brows lifted in surprise. 'I wonder why not. I like reading recipes, which makes me think that I must've enjoyed cooking at some stage of my life,' she told him, walking into a breathtaking bedroom as complete in charm and appeal as the ground-floor reception areas. Turning round, her head tilted back to appreciate the vaulted ceiling above, she sped through the door into the corner turret room to laugh in delight when her suspicions proved correct and she discovered a deftly arranged circular bathroom. 'It's a wonderful house, Lorenzo. Was it a wreck when you found it?'

'A complete ruin,' he confirmed. 'I loved the views and the old courtyard out the back, which was completely overgrown. I didn't really appreciate how much potential the house itself had or, indeed, how large it was. We certainly don't require the half-dozen bedrooms we have here.'

The doors had been secured back on a balcony on the opposite wall and she strolled out, relieved the ironwork was thick enough to prevent a nosy little dog from sliding between bars and falling, because there was no use pretending, she thought fondly, Topsy wasn't the brightest or most cautious spark on the planet. Seconds later she was so enthralled by the view of the Tuscan landscape, she simply stared.

A hint of early morning mist still hung over the picturesque walled stone village on a nearby hilltop and somehow it almost magically enhanced the lush green of the vines and fruit orchards in the valley below. Ancient spreading chestnut trees marked the boundary of the garden, the turning colour of their leaves hinting that autumn was on its way. 'It's really beautiful,' she sighed.

The only outstandingly beautiful object in his vision at that moment, Lorenzo acknowledged abstractedly, was her, a foam of curls falling naturally across her bare shoulders in a white-blonde mass, the pretty, surprisingly simple blue dress only adding to the fragile femininity that she exuded and the slender, shapely legs on view. Hunger stabbed through him as sharp and immediate in its penetration as a knife and he strode forward.

Brooke relaxed back into the warmth of his lean powerful frame as his hand came down on her shoulder, a roaring readiness within her taut body to do whatever it took to ensure that their relationship had a fighting chance of survival. His sensual mouth dropped a kiss down on her other shoulder and she trembled, her body coming alive as though he had pressed a magic switch, and by the time he shifted his lips to the considerably more sensitive flesh of the slope leading up to her neck, her hips were pushing back against his in helpless response.

The zip of her dress eased slowly down and he spread the parted edges to run his mouth down over her slender back and she wriggled and jerked, learning that she had tender spots she had not known she possessed. The snap of her bra being released unnerved her when she was standing out in the fresh air, *in public*, as she saw it, even though it was a very rural area. She spun in his arms.

'I don't want anyone to see me,' she mumbled nervously, suddenly wondering if that reaction was a passion killer as he looked down at her in seeming surprise at her inhibitions. 'I mean, there might be…er…workers in the vines or something.'

Lorenzo laughed soft and low and swept her up into his arms as if she were a lightweight, when she knew she was not, and carried her over to the bed. He skimmed off her bra with almost daunting expertise. Her violet eyes shot up to lock to his lean bronzed face. 'You must've been with an awful lot of women,' she heard herself say, and five seconds later cringed at that revealing observation, her face burning as hot as hellfire.

Taken aback, Lorenzo looked down at her in surprise. 'The usual number before we married,' he conceded.

'And not…er…*since*?' Brooke prompted, unable to stifle that question. 'I mean…we were separated…and then I was in a coma for well over a year…'

'I haven't been with anyone else since the day I married you,' Lorenzo spelt out with a level of precision that disconcerted her even more. 'I don't break my promises.'

A controversial topic, she recognised uneasily, but she was impressed nonetheless by that steadfast fidelity that many men would surely have forsaken during a legal separation. It was one more gift to appreciate, wasn't it? In one statement he had both surprised and delighted her, affirming her conviction that they might still have a marriage worth saving. He had not turned to another woman for either sex or consolation and that said so much about the sort of guy he was. She wanted to tell him that she loved him again, but she swallowed the words, which would strike him as empty when she didn't have the luxury of even recalling their past relationship.

'We're getting too serious,' Lorenzo told her with a sudden flashing smile that didn't quite reach his gorgeous eyes.

'Blame me,' she muttered ruefully. 'I was the one asking awkward questions.'

'You should feel free to say whatever you like to me,' Lorenzo told her, backing away from the bed to slam the door shut and shed his jacket, his tie and his shoes in rapid succession.

Brooke swallowed hard, wondering why she always felt so shy with him, wondering why she wanted to cover her bared breasts from view. She *had* to be accustomed to such intimacy. That she could be innately shy in the bedroom, after all, went against everything she had so far learned about herself. Women who were shy or modest about showing their bodies didn't wear teeny-tiny shorts and incredibly short skirts, she reminded herself impatiently.

There was nothing shy about Lorenzo either, she acknowledged as he strolled, buck naked, back to the bed like a very, *very* sexy bronzed predator, all lean, rippling muscle and hair-roughened thighs. Just looking at Lorenzo almost overwhelmed her because she still experienced a deep, abiding sense of wonder that such a rich, powerful and important man had married her. Yet where did that low self-esteem come from? She was supposed to be so confident, a woman in possession of a trust fund, both prosperous and successful in her own right. Had she always been scared on the inside and confident on the outside?

'*Dio*... I can't wait to get inside you,' Lorenzo growled.

That graphic assurance sent a flush running right up over her breasts into her face and that out-of-her-depth sensation that had grabbed her on the only night she had so far spent with him returned.

'What's wrong?' Lorenzo scanned the rapid changing expressions on her taut face. 'And why have you turned red?'

'I don't know,' Brooke gabbled, suddenly snaking free of the dress round her hips and kicking off her shoes to scramble below the sheets, desperate to be doing something rather than freezing guiltily beneath that far too shrewd and clever gaze of his. He picked up on her insecurities and it was not only embarrassing but also unnerving because it stripped away what little poise she retained.

'You're blushing!' Lorenzo laughed in apparent appreciation of that achievement.

'Did you have to mention it?' Brooke groaned. 'To me, being with you like this still feels very *new*. I know that's silly but that's how it is.'

'No, it's not silly. I'm being insensitive,' Lorenzo sliced in with lingering incomprehension at the concept of Brooke being embarrassed about anything on the planet. But he could see that, as far as she was concerned, she was telling him the truth and once again he marvelled at the transparency of her expressions.

'I'm the one out of step here with the norm, not you.' Brooke stretched up a hand to grasp his, trying to bridge the gap between them.

Lorenzo ceased trying to wrap his head around the inexplicable and came down on the bed to rub an appreciative hand over a succulent pink nipple and close his mouth there instead. When had she got so serious? When had *he* begun to behave as though what was only a temporary identity were the *real* Brooke? She was driving him insane again, only it was in a very different way from the first time around, he conceded fiercely. Here he was craving his almost exwife like an addictive drug. For the first time since the crash he wanted to walk away… and then her fingers tightened round his and she looked up at him and she smiled, and his thoughts evaporated as though they had never existed.

She stretched up, clumsily gripping his arm for support, and settled her ripe pink lips against his and the scent of her, the sweet delicious taste of her as her tongue darted against his, turned Lorenzo on so hard and fast, he flattened her down to the bed with two strong hands, his dominant nature taking over with all the passion he had once had to restrain in the marital bed. But there were no curbs now and he could not resist that lure of being himself for the first time with her or the temptation of not being with a woman who lay back like a goddess inviting worship and never touched him.

Brooke felt the change in him and welcomed his passion, realising that she had almost frightened him off with her insecurities. Her fingers delved into his luxuriant black hair and smoothed down his high cheekbones to the roughened blue shadow of stubble that highlighted his wide sensual mouth. She gasped as he dipped his head over her breasts and seized a swollen pink crest and grazed it with the edge of his teeth. She was *so* sensitive there that her back arched and then his skilled hands were travelling lower, tracing the damp cleft between her thighs, probing the tight entrance, making her hips rock up and a low-pitched cry part her lips.

'You're so ready for me,' Lorenzo husked in satisfaction, shifting position to roll her over and up onto her knees.

Her whole body clenched in sensual shock as he drove into her hard and fast. It was electrifying, every skin cell and nerve ending in her body powering the excitement that made her heart race and her breath catch in her throat. Every sleek, powerful thrust of his body sent sensation tumbling and cascading in seismic waves through her quivering body and heightened the tight clenching low in her pelvis. Her internal muscles contracted and sent her careening with a cry into a climax that detonated like a bomb of sheer pleasure inside her trembling body. It felt so good tears of reaction burned her eyes and she blinked rapidly. But he wasn't finished, no, far from it, and as the pressure began to build and tighten unbearably inside her again, it only took one expert touch at the most sensitive spot in her body for another orgasm to fly through her in a violent storm.

Shattered, she collapsed down on the bed, while he groaned in satisfaction and his arms tightened round her, flipping her round so that his wicked mouth could tease her parted lips and then slide between, sending a quivering tremor through her drained length.

'Not moving for anything ever again,' she swore limply.

'The helicopter's picking me up at two but I'll be back by nine this evening,' Lorenzo intoned, brilliant dark eyes connecting with hers. 'Sleep this afternoon because you won't be getting much sleep tonight, *cara mia.*'

'Promises, promises,' Brooke teased, feeling wonderfully relaxed. 'You could be absolutely exhausted.'

Lorenzo smoothed her tumbled curls off her pale brow and curled her slight length close. 'I won't be too tired for you,' he intoned huskily, purposely closing off every logical thought and living in the moment. *She* was doing that and if he wasn't prepared to let her go yet, so must he.

Four weeks later, after Lorenzo had repeatedly extended their stay, Brooke stood back to study the table she had laid on the terrace at the side of the house. She was humming under her breath as she walked back into the kitchen to check the bubbling pots. Tonight, she was cooking because Sofia was away visiting her daughter but she wasn't quite as adept a cook as she had hoped when she first came up with the idea of providing dinner. Sofia, however, had given her some useful tips and some even more useful short-cuts and, with a little preparation and help behind the scenes beforehand, Brooke had felt able to tackle a simple menu.

She glanced at the tiny half-knitted garment that Sofia had left lying on the dresser. The older woman was knitting a cardigan for her first grandchild. Brooke picked it up, unable to explain why it had attracted her attention in the first place as she found herself scanning the intricate pattern, and then registered that she could name every one of the stitches used and even identify a mistake. She blinked and something tugged almost painfully deep within her brain. She shook her head again in surprise. So, she knew how to knit, like lots of other people, she acknowledged dismissively, and rubbed her brow until the tightness there began to evaporate.

As she walked back out to the terrace, a bout of unnerving dizziness made her head swim and her legs falter and she swiftly took a seat, lowered her head and breathed in deep and slow. She didn't know what was amiss with her and already planned to visit a doctor when they flew back to London the following day. She didn't think that the faintness or the headache were linked to her head injury, any more than the nausea that had assailed her at odd moments in recent days, but she thought it was time that she had herself checked out all the same. Perhaps she was coming down with some virus, she thought ruefully.

A slim figure in white cropped jeans and a vest top, she stood up again and studied the view of the tranquil patchwork of vines and orchards and fields that spread out beyond the garden boundaries. She had never dreamt that they would end up staying an entire month in Italy and the time had fairly raced past. Lorenzo had flown off to loads of business meetings but every other day he was at home, either working or taking her out somewhere, and their peaceful stay had done wonders for her state of mind.

Regrettably, she had experienced no further flashbacks, which was a considerable disappointment to her, but, on the balance side, she was sleeping well, eating well and generally felt much stronger. A lot of that related to her improved relationship with Lorenzo though, she conceded. He hadn't promised to make a special effort when he had said that they would see how their marriage went but he had definitely been trying.

Regardless of how busy he was, he had made time for her. She had drunk a glass of the local wine in the Piazza Grande in Montepulciano, strolled under the trees by the walls of Lucca, explored the labyrinth of underground caves in Pitigliano and wandered silent in appreciation through the gardens of Garzoni in Collodi. There had been dinners out as well in wonderful restaurants in Florence, but she had enjoyed the picnic in the orange orchard below the house even more because Lorenzo had surprised her with a sapphire pendant that took her breath away and had then made passionate love to her.

She had never felt so close to anyone as she felt to Lorenzo, and sometimes it scared her because she knew that she wasn't in a safe or settled marriage and that, at any time, Lorenzo could again decide that he wanted a divorce. When she allowed herself to think along those lines, her nervous tension went sky-high and so she tried to enjoy what they currently had without thinking too far ahead into the future. She didn't tell him she loved him now, no longer dared to be that confiding. Had she known the true state of their marriage, she would never have said it in the first place. She didn't want Lorenzo to feel trapped or that he couldn't tell her the truth, and her telling him that she loved him could only make him feel uncomfortable.

By the time the helicopter landed, Brooke had laid out the first course on the table and she stood back, smiling, as Lorenzo strode up the slope towards her, eye-catchingly gorgeous in his exquisitely tailored dove-grey suit, his luxuriant black hair ruffled, his spectacular dark golden eyes locked to her.

And, truth to tell, there was not a single cloud on Lorenzo's horizon at that moment and his lean, dark, serious face flashed into a smile at the sight of her waiting for him. It probably made him a four-letter word of a guy but he enjoyed the knowledge that his wife's world seemed to revolve entirely around him. She was a slender but curvy figure dressed entirely in white, her cloud of curls framing her piquant features, eyes purple as violets.

'I made dinner,' Brooke announced. 'But you have to sit down now.'

Lorenzo tensed. 'I was heading for a shower first—'

'You can't...if you do that the main course will be ready too soon and it will spoil,' Brooke told him earnestly. 'If you want to eat, it's now or never.'

Lorenzo grinned. 'I'll make a bargain with you. I sit down now to eat, and you join me in the shower afterwards...'

'That's a deal.' Brooke went pink and sank down at the other side of the table. 'Dig in. It's quite a simple meal but this timing thing is complicated.'

'I can't believe you've made a meal for us,' Lorenzo confided truthfully.

'It may not win any awards but I think I should be able to make a decent meal,' Brooke contended seriously. 'It's a basic skill.'

'How are you feeling about returning to London tomorrow?' he prompted.

'Kind of sad,' she confided, laying down her fork to finger the sapphire gleaming below her collarbone. 'I love it here and I've relaxed a lot more but we can't live cut off from the rest of the world for ever.'

'No, we can't,' Lorenzo agreed and, as he

pushed his plate away to indicate that he was finished, he lounged back in his chair and spread his hands. 'Why did you go to all this trouble for a meal? We could've eaten out. That's what I usually do when Sofia takes a night off.'

'It's our last night here.' Brooke shrugged in an effort to be casual and pushed back her chair to return to the kitchen. There she drained pans, whisked the sauce again and put the main course together on delicate china plates to take them out to the table.

'It looks great,' Lorenzo said softly.

'Wait and see how it tastes,' she urged.

He ate in deliberate silence, cleared the plate and then sent her a wicked grin of appreciation. 'That's it. You're on kitchen duty every night that I can spare you.'

'And how often would you spare me?' she enquired as she pushed her own plate away and went to fetch dessert.

'Not very often,' Lorenzo confessed, following her into the kitchen to tug her back against his lean, hard frame, his hands smoothing down over her hip bones to lace across her flat stomach. 'You have a much more important role to fulfil, *cara mia*.'

Insanely aware that he was aroused, she instinctively pressed back into him, loving the sudden fracture in his breathing and the way his fingers instantly slid up to the waistband of her jeans to release the button and delve down over her quivering tummy to the heart of her. 'And what would that role entail?' she prompted shakily, suspecting that he wasn't likely to let her make it as far as dessert.

Interpreting the damp welcome below her silk knickers, not to mention the encouraging gasp parting her lips, Lorenzo laughed appreciatively. 'I think you already know, *gatita mia*.'

'Well, you *have* to make a choice. Me...' Brooke told him, battling her hunger for him to gently step away and fasten her jeans, 'or the last course.'

Lorenzo snatched her back to him. 'I'm Italian...the woman wins every time.'

'Maybe *if* you're really, really good,' Brooke teased, 'I'll bring you dessert in bed.'

In answer, Lorenzo spun her round and kissed her with voracious hunger, his mouth crushing hers, one hand anchored in her mass of curls. Beneath that onslaught, she gasped and he wasted no time in bending down to scoop her up and head for the stairs. 'Bossy...*much*?' she taunted.

'You know you like it,' Lorenzo breathed with inherent dark sensuality, dropping her down on the bed and following her there to pluck off her shoes and divest her of the rest of her clothes.

'No, you undress first,' Brooke instructed, feeling daring as she pushed his jacket off his broad shoulders and yanked at his tie, her fingers deft on his shirt buttons. Pushing the fabric back, she spread her hands over the warm hair-roughened musculature of his chest.

Lorenzo vaulted off the bed to remove the rest of his clothes. 'Off with the jeans and the top,' he commanded impatiently.

Brooke made a production of shimmying out of her tight jeans, sliding out one slender bare leg, then the next. Bending back, she released the hooks on her top and peeled it off over her head, her teeth tightening at the over-sensitivity of her engorged nipples as the air stung them. Her breasts had felt weird for several days, tender and swollen, and she had thought that had to be a sign of her menstrual cycle kicking in. Although she had had periods while she was still in the clinic, she had not had one since she left medical care and she knew that she would have to mention that to the doctor when she saw him as well. Possibly that IUD Lorenzo had mentioned was causing her problems, she reasoned wryly, and perhaps she would have to consider another method of birth control.

Lorenzo feasted his eyes on her with unashamed appreciation, his attention lingering on the luscious swell of her breasts. She must've put on weight and it really, really suited her, he acknowledged hungrily. 'I'm burning up for you—'

'Since when? You woke me up at six this morning,' Brooke reminded him helplessly, as always, almost astonished by his constant desire for her.

Lorenzo grinned and came down beside her. 'That was this morning and it was a lifetime ago, *bellezza mia*.'

'Will we still be like this when we go home?' Brooke heard herself ask in sudden fear that their new intimacy would somehow vanish when they left Italy.

'You're moving into my bedroom,' Lorenzo asserted.

'Am I?' Brooke smiled like a cat that had got the cream, reassured by that statement, that change in attitude that signified togetherness rather than separation.

'Are you thinking of arguing about that?' Lorenzo husked against her reddened mouth.

Her fingers speared into his black hair to draw him down to her, the same intense hunger firing through every atom of her being. 'No.'

A long while later, she lay in perfect peace in his arms and drifted off to sleep in a happy daze, which made the dream that followed all the more frightening because she wasn't prepared for it, couldn't *ever* have been prepared for the images that went flashing through her brain and made her scream so loud in the dark that she hurt her throat.

She saw the crash. She saw Brooke as she reached for her and failed to catch her hand, experienced the agony of knowing she had *failed* to save her sister, her only living relative. And in the shaken aftermath, when she must have regained consciousness for a split second, reliving that unimaginable pain and primal fear, she saw her knitting needles strewn in the smoking wreckage of the car...

'It's OK...it's OK...' Lorenzo soothed as she sat bolt upright in the bed, rocking back and forth, her head down on her raised knees as she sobbed. 'You had a nightmare. It's not real, none of it's real. *Dio*, you screamed so loudly I thought we were being attacked!'

But it was real, it was *very* real, Milly recognised, her frantic thoughts tangled and befogged by layer after layer of shock and growing disbelief. Somehow she had got her memory back, the memory she had once been so desperate to retrieve. Her true self had slipped back without fanfare into place during that nightmare, clarifying everything that had previously been a complete blank. But, disturbingly, reclaiming her memory and her knowledge of who she was had plunged her into an even more frightening world.

Brooke was dead and she was devastated by that knowledge, even though the last time she had been with her half-sister she had finally appreciated that Brooke was unlikely ever to accept her as a true sibling. But it was one thing to accept that, another entirely to accept that Brooke was now gone for ever and that their relationship could never be improved.

Her sister was dead and Milly had been mistaken for her. How had that happened? But the more she thought about it, the easier it became to understand. After all, she had been wearing Brooke's jewellery and Brooke's clothes and she had had facial injuries. The strong resemblance between the two women had gone completely unnoticed, presumably because Brooke had been seriously injured too. Her reddened eyes stung with fresh tears.

How on earth could she ever put right all that had gone wrong?

Lorenzo would be devastated.

Lorenzo didn't even know he was a widower. How could he? He had spent months looking after his injured wife's needs, caring for her because she had no one else and then, ultimately, living with and having sex with the woman he naturally believed to be his wife. But she *wasn't* his wife, she was a stranger, just as he had been a stranger to her when she first wakened out of the coma. Only, sadly, neither of them had recognised that reality.

Trembling, retreating fast from Lorenzo's attempts to soothe her, she hurried into the bathroom, for once taking no pleasure in her surroundings. She ran a bath as an excuse to stay there alone. Lorenzo appeared in the doorway, tall, dark and bronzed, and she chased him off again, telling him she just needed a warm bath and a little space to relax. Tears ran down her cheeks then as she sat in the warm water, all the mistakes she had made piling up on top of her, and she didn't know, she really didn't know *how* to go about telling Lorenzo the truth. He had said nothing was real in her nightmare, but he was wrong—it was all *too* real and the harsh facts could not be ignored. She had wakened from a nightmare to find herself entangled in a worse nightmare, because she was living her dead sister's life with a man she loved, who did not love her. Lorenzo was wrong: nothing was OK and it never would be again...

CHAPTER EIGHT

'DON'T TELL ME that you're fine again,' Lorenzo warned her in a raw-edged undertone, his lean, darkly handsome features set in stern lines as the limo wafted them through the London traffic from the airport. 'Obviously you're anything but fine. Something has upset you a great deal and it's time that you shared it with me.'

'We'll talk when we get back…er…home,' she told him shakily, in no hurry to get there and deal with his outrage, his disbelief and his belated grief.

Lorenzo had never been hers and her tummy lurched at the knowledge that everything that had happened between them had been based purely on his conviction that she was his wife. His *every* word, his *every* decision, his *every* caress had been bestowed on Brooke, not Milly, she reminded herself doggedly, shrinking guiltily from the knowledge that *she* had encouraged *him* into sharing a bed. Brooke had hated Lorenzo, she reminded herself, reluctantly thinking back to her sibling's conviction that Lorenzo was a possessive tyrant, who had unjustly accused her of infidelity in order to divorce her.

Obviously there had been a great deal of bitterness in their relationship by that stage. But Milly liked to think that, had Brooke seen how very supportive Lorenzo had been in the wake of the crash to the woman he believed to be his wife, she would have forgiven him for their differences. On that score, his behaviour had been above reproach. He could've walked away, let the divorce go ahead, leaving her to the tender mercies of the healthcare system and some legal executor. But Lorenzo hadn't done that. He had stood by the vows he had once taken…*in sickness and in health.*

Her head was aching again with all the stress of her feverish thoughts and she rubbed her brow, wishing foolishly that there were some miraculous way of avoiding what lay ahead of her. Obviously, she would have to leave Lorenzo's house and as soon as possible. Unfortunately for her, she had nowhere to go and not a penny to her name and no close friends either, because she had moved around too much to form lasting friendships.

It was a shame that she hadn't worked harder at the many different schools she had attended during her years in foster care, she reflected with regret. Sadly, the knowledge that she would inevitably be shifted to a new foster home and a new school with different exam boards and course content had removed any enthusiasm she had had when she was younger for studying. The continual changes had made her unsettled, undisciplined and distrustful of forging close relationships with anyone because, sooner or later, everyone seemed to leave her and move on.

Perhaps that was why she had repressed every qualm to stay friendly and involved with Brooke, generally accepting whatever treatment Brooke dealt out. She hadn't wanted to lose that all-important link with Brooke and had been eager to offer her half-sister all her love and support. Hadn't she clung to Lorenzo in much the same way? Pathetically eager to offer love even when he wasn't looking for it? Inside herself, she cringed for her weakness and susceptibility. But then had she *ever* been loved?

Her memories of her mother were very hazy because Natalia had died when Milly was only eleven years old, but Natalia *had* been affectionate and caring. Her father, however, had never paid her any attention when he visited them, hadn't seemed to have the slightest interest in her, she recalled sadly, although possibly his apparent indifference had come from his guilt at cheating on his wife. Had her mother not told her that William Jackson was her father, she would never have known because his name wasn't on her birth certificate. Although he had supported her mother financially, he had refused to officially acknowledge Milly as his daughter.

'We're home,' Lorenzo imparted flatly.

But Madrigal Court was *his* home, not hers, Milly ruminated, and immediately wanted to kick herself for that forlorn thought. Like many children raised by the state, she had always longed for a stable and permanent home. It was not a bit of wonder that when she had been deprived of her memory that deep-based need had surfaced and made her latch onto Brooke's home and husband like a homing pigeon eager to find a permanent roost.

'I'm afraid I can't understand how a bad dream can cause you this much stress,' Lorenzo breathed impatiently as he herded her into the pristine white drawing room and closed the door behind them. 'What on earth is the matter?'

Milly breathed in deep and slow to steady her nerves. 'I remembered the accident,' she admitted. 'And then my memory came back.'

Lorenzo paled and his lean, powerful frame went rigid. 'Just like that?'

'Just like that,' she confirmed sickly. 'But the real problem is that when I regained my memory I realised that I'm not the person everyone assumed I was...'

His brow pleated as if he was still trying to penetrate the meaning of that statement. 'What are you talking about?'

'I'm not Brooke Tassini, Lorenzo. I'm *not* your wife. I'm Milly Taylor.'

The fringe of his lush black lashes shot up over incredulous dark golden eyes and then he swung round and headed back to the door, pulling out his phone. 'That's not possible.'

'Where are you going?' she gasped.

Lorenzo compressed his lips. It was obvious to him that his wife was having some sort of nervous breakdown. He had not a clue how to deal with such an astonishing statement, but he was convinced that her psychiatrist would know. 'I'm contacting Mr Selby so that you can discuss this with him.'

'I don't want to see Mr Selby right now. I need to get things straight with you first,' Milly declared tautly. 'That's more important.'

'There *is* nothing more important than your mental health,' Lorenzo contradicted, sending her a censorious glance from his position by the door. 'Why did you keep quiet about this? Why didn't you immediately tell me what you were going through last night?'

'I had to get my head straight,' she protested. 'It was a big shock for me too and I feel terrible about everything that's happened. I don't know how the heck you'll ever sort out all the legal stuff.'

An imperious ebony brow elevated. 'What legal stuff?'

Milly dragged in another steadying breath. 'Brooke's... Brooke's dead, Lorenzo, and I've been declared dead but I'm still alive. That mistake will have to be rectified...*somehow*.'

Lorenzo was holding his phone so tightly between his fingers that he almost crushed it. Was she suffering from what he had heard referred to as a psychotic break? He studied her pale, rigid face, reading her distress. She really *believed* this stuff she was telling him, he registered in consternation: she had decided that she was not his wife, that she was the other woman in the car. Why would she do that?

'Brooke was my sister,' she murmured tautly.

'Brooke doesn't have a sister,' he overruled.

'Not officially. I'm illegitimate,' Milly admitted stiffly. 'William Jackson had an affair that went on for years with my mother and I was born during their affair. He never recognised me as his child and never treated me as if I was his and I didn't know back then that he was a married man with another family. Brooke traced me and came to see me out of curiosity when I was eighteen and just leaving foster care. She was my half-sister...'

Lorenzo released his breath in a slow, measured hiss. He hadn't had Milly Taylor's birth and background checked out, hadn't considered her past relevant in establishing who she had been to his wife. He could not yet accept the enormity of what he was being told but he also could not imagine how or why his wife could have come up with such a detailed and fanciful story overnight.

'Brooke would've mentioned a sister.'

'She didn't tell anyone about me and was careful never to be seen in public with me. My very existence was...' Milly hesitated before forging on with a frown '...pretty much a source of resentment and annoyance to her. She knew about the affair and the amount of unhappiness it had caused *her* mother. My mother was dead by the time Brooke sought me out, but I suspect that the bitter anger she felt towards my mother transferred to me to some extent.'

Lorenzo was frowning. 'A half-sister? But that doesn't explain anything! If Brooke didn't like you or find you useful in some way, what would you have been doing in that car with her on the day of the crash? Nothing about this story makes sense!'

Milly stood up slowly, her violet eyes deeply troubled. 'I can help it make sense but you have to try to keep your temper.'

Lorenzo flung his arrogant dark head back and dealt her a scorching appraisal. 'Of course, I can keep my temper, but I still don't think you're going to be able to explain this nonsense, and discussing it as if it's true fact isn't helping the situation or you.'

'Brooke used me as her stand-in on several occasions,' Milly admitted starkly. 'We looked very alike, even more alike after I had had cosmetic surgery done on my nose,' she continued doggedly as Lorenzo continued to stare at her as though she had sprouted horns and cloven hooves. 'Brooke paid for the procedure and I didn't want to get it done but when I said no, she dropped me, and I was so desperate to hang onto our relationship that eventually I agreed.'

Lorenzo was frowning in disbelief. 'You looked alike? What was wrong with your nose?'

'It was too big. Nobody would have mistaken me for her if I hadn't agreed to the surgery. After that, she used me a couple of times to stand in for her at charity events where I didn't have to do much pretending. I'm no actress,' she confided tightly. 'Sometimes, she didn't want to attend events or she wanted to mislead the press about where she was and then she would phone me up and ask me to go in her place. She would give me her clothes and her jewellery to wear.'

His frown had laced his bone structure with hard lines of tension. 'You are telling me that you engaged in deception with Brooke to trick other people, including me?'

Milly bridled. 'That isn't how I saw it and you were never involved. I was just helping my sister out. Smoothing out her life when she was too busy to meet all the demands on her time,' she protested.

'You were deceiving people,' Lorenzo contradicted with glacial disapproval. 'If this far-fetched story is true, tell me where you were going on the day of the crash.'

Milly winced. 'I was to go to a hotel and stay there for several days pretending to be Brooke while she was away somewhere on holiday, having travelled on my passport. But, of course, we never got as far as the hotel or the airport...'

'She was using *your* passport?' Lorenzo demanded incredulously. 'But that's illegal! Where was she going?'

'I don't know. She didn't tell me,' Milly replied numbly. 'Sometimes she told me stuff, sometimes, she told me nothing. It depended on her mood.'

And that *was* a startlingly accurate description of Brooke's unpredictable, temperamental nature, Lorenzo conceded grudgingly, because in spite of all logic he was beginning to listen, beginning to put facts together to finally see a picture forming that could make some kind of sense. He could certainly check out whether a Milly Taylor had failed to turn up for her flight that day and he could look deeper into her background to see if he could establish an official link that would bear out her story.

From Milly's point of view, Lorenzo's attitude seemed oddly detached. He was dealing with the facts, avoiding the harsher realities of their situation, she suspected ruefully.

'Well, anyway,' she mumbled. 'That's what I was doing in the limo on the day of the crash. Brooke gave me the clothes she was wearing and her jewellery and I put them on while she got changed. I expect that is how I came to be identified as her.'

'You were unrecognisable,' Lorenzo admitted starkly, shifting his attention away from her as if he could no longer bear to look at her, his big, powerful frame rigid. 'You are telling me that my wife is dead, that she actually died eighteen months ago in the accident...'

'I'm so sorry. I'm sorry about everything that's happened!' Milly muttered in a driven rush of regret. 'If I hadn't been suffering from amnesia, I could have identified myself and you would have known the truth months ago...'

Lorenzo expelled his breath and raked a long-fingered brown hand roughly through his cropped black hair, his emotional turmoil palpable. 'Brooke is gone...'

'Yes,' Milly whispered, tears lashing her eyes. 'Do you believe me now?'

'Only once I have had time to confirm the extraordinary facts you have given me,' Lorenzo told her flatly.

Milly suppressed a shudder, feeling dismissed, sidelined, set back at a new and disturbing distance from him while he worked out whether she was a fantasist or a woman having a breakdown. All of a sudden everything had changed between them. Lorenzo was changing before her very eyes. It was as though their personal relationship had never happened, she acknowledged painfully. But then it had all been a lie, based on the false premise that Brooke was still alive, and at this moment Lorenzo was fathoms deep in shock and struggling to deal with the reality that his wife was dead. That was all he had the ability to consider right now and how could she expect anything more from him?

She studied his tall dark figure and the forbidding tension locking his facial muscles tight. It was selfish of her to feel rejected by his new reserve when she had no claim on him or his attention. She was nothing to him, never had been. Everything he had done for her had really been done for Brooke. On his terms she didn't really exist. And now that he knew that she *did* exist, he would never touch her again and would never look at her again as he once had.

And she had to deal with that reality and come back down to earth again, which would be challenging. After all, she had been living a kind of fantasy life with Lorenzo, a waitress from a very ordinary background, suddenly swept off into a billionaire's luxury lifestyle with private jets, servants and a level of wealth and comfort previously beyond her imagining. But it wasn't those expensive trappings she would miss, she conceded wretchedly, it would be Lorenzo.

Lorenzo, whom she loved to pieces, who didn't want her any more, who would never want her again. She felt as though her heart were breaking in two inside her and, tensing her slight shoulders, she compressed her lips, determined not to say or do anything emotional. Right now, Lorenzo didn't need that added stress and probably didn't even want to recall that he had had sex with her believing that she was his wife. No, the faster she got back out of his life again, the happier Lorenzo would be.

Lorenzo was looking back down through the months and marvelling that he had allowed the medics to silence his every misgiving about the woman who had come out of the coma. From her first wakening every atom of his ESP and intelligence had combined to send him continual warnings that Brooke's personality and character had apparently changed out of all recognition. He had listened to the doctors because it had naturally never occurred to him that the woman in the convalescent clinic could be anyone other than his wife.

Dio mio, she had been identified as his wife at the scene of the crash, presented to him as his wife when he was handed her jewellery for safekeeping before surgery. That an appalling mistake could've been made had not once crossed his mind or anyone else's. How could it have done when nobody had been aware of the striking resemblance between the two women? Of course, he hadn't had access either to her clarifying explanation about the nature of her relationship with Brooke. Brooke, indeed, had probably only latched onto her half-sister in the first place because of that resemblance, seeing how she could use that to her advantage. Milly had been acting as Brooke's stand-in, her *lookalike*. Distaste with her for having taken on such a deceptive role flared inside him, chilling his hard dark eyes to granite.

'I'll move out as soon as I can,' Milly muttered in a rush.

'Where are you planning to go?' Lorenzo lifted an ebony brow. 'Straight to the press to sell the story of the century for a fat price?'

Milly was aghast that he could even harbour such a suspicion and she turned white as milk, her violet eyes standing out stark against her porcelain skin. 'Of course not! I wouldn't do that to you or me.'

'Not even for the money?' Lorenzo prompted doubtingly.

Lorenzo's brain was awash with disconnected confused thoughts. He could not yet process what he had just learned. He struggled looking back through the long months with the woman he had believed to be his wife and accepting that she was an entirely different woman. And a stranger, his logic chipped in. A complete and total stranger. He grasped that he needed time and peace to come to terms with what he had just learned.

Milly went rigid, struggling to credit that only the night before Lorenzo had been making passionate love to her and holding her close in the aftermath as if she meant something to him. 'No, not even for the money,' she said sickly.

Lorenzo swung away from her as he could no longer stand to look at her. 'Pack,' he instructed grimly, recognising that he had to immediately get her out of the house if he was to avoid a sordid scandal. 'I have somewhere for you to live sitting ready for occupation and you might as well live there. Once I've checked out the information you've given me and consulted my lawyers, we'll sort this mess out.'

Pack?

Pure shock resonated through Milly and momentarily her head swam, and she felt dizzy. Evidently, he couldn't wait to get rid of her and the immediacy of his demand that she pack and move out disconcerted her. She might have told herself that he would want her to leave as soon as possible but her mind had yet to accept that idea. She hadn't been prepared for that change to take place so quickly and she blinked rapidly, her eyes dazed.

'I have nothing to pack. I don't own anything here,' she said flatly, because it was true when she didn't even own the clothes she wore because he had paid for everything.

'Don't be ridiculous!' Lorenzo growled. '*Anything* you have worn, *anything* that you have been using, is yours to take with you. Brooke is gone and she's not coming back.'

Milly nodded jerkily and quickly stood up, the dizziness she was still enduring dampening her face with perspiration. She felt ill, nauseous, but that was a weakness she had to hide. Lorenzo might be throwing her out but she was not about to play the poor little victim who couldn't cope. She had had enough of being weak and vulnerable while she was still in medical care.

As she opened the door to leave, Topsy hurled herself at her knees in greeting.

'You can take the dog with you too,' Lorenzo murmured. 'She's got used to you now. It would be cruel to separate you.'

But, seemingly, it wasn't cruel to kick out a bogus wife at such short notice, Milly reflected, heading upstairs with a straight spine, still battling to hold the dizziness at bay. Some sort of stupid virus she couldn't shake off, she thought wearily. As soon as she got settled, she would go and see a doctor, she promised herself. The clothes she had worn in Italy were still in the cases they had returned in and not yet unpacked, but even as she started to assemble the few items that she hadn't taken abroad with her, a maid arrived with empty cases for her to use. Lorenzo had already told the staff that she was leaving and her still-sensitive stomach rebelled to send her racing into the en suite to be sick.

Afterwards, she cleaned her teeth and with all the animation of a robot she went back to doggedly packing. She didn't have very much to show for her months in Lorenzo's life. She stripped off the rings, the diamond-studded watch and the sapphire pendant and laid them on the dressing table because they weren't hers, or at least had been gifts that weren't intended for her.

She might feel as though her life were over but, really, it was only beginning another phase, she tried to tell herself. Being hurt that Lorenzo wanted her out of his house was foolish. He had to mourn Brooke and adjust to the knowledge that the wife he had watched over for months while she was in a coma had not survived as he had believed. He had to draw a line under the past months and obviously he didn't want her around while he was trying to do that.

The cases were stowed in the limo and Milly climbed into the passenger seat, clutching Topsy to her like a tiny hairy comfort blanket. Lorenzo emerged last from the house, his lean, darkly handsome face wiped clean of emotion or any form of warmth, and barely a word was exchanged during the drive into London.

It was a fabulous apartment with its own private lift. Milly stood looking around her at the sea of crisp white furnishings and swallowed apprehensively.

'I had it decorated for Brooke,' Lorenzo

breathed in a roughened undertone. 'She loved it.'

'It's spectacular,' she said woodenly, wanting him to leave so that she could ditch her game face. But at the same time, she was dreading the moment when he would actually leave and already wondering how long it would be before she saw him again.

'It's yours now. You can make any changes you want…at my expense,' he added impatiently when she glanced at him in astonishment. 'Legally, this will ultimately be *your* apartment.'

Milly frowned in bewilderment. 'How on earth could it ever be mine?' she queried.

'I signed it over to Brooke before the accident and, according to my lawyers, everything that once belonged to Brooke is likely to go to you in the end because I refused to take it. I don't want anything that belonged to her,' he confessed quietly. 'Of course, it will take weeks, if not months, to disentangle the legal threads concerning the misidentification that has been made and free up her funds. In the meantime I will ensure that you are financially secure. The apartment is serviced. The fridge should be packed with food.'

'I don't want your money,' she whispered and flinched inside herself because standing in an apartment he had bought, wearing clothing he had purchased and making such a statement struck her as absurd. But the knowledge that he had evidently consulted his lawyers about their situation before she had even left his home chilled her to the marrow.

'Nonetheless, I will not leave you destitute. That would be unpardonable,' Lorenzo bit out in a fierce undertone. 'You have done nothing wrong. In your role as Brooke's lookalike you may have innocently contributed to the mistaken identification that was made but your life has been disrupted as much as mine by what happened. It's my responsibility to ensure that you don't suffer for that.'

Milly was already suffering, and she didn't want to hear that he still viewed her as his responsibility, not when he was in the act of casting her off like an old shoe. Her stomach lurched again and she crossed her arms defensively. She said nothing while she watched him from below her lashes, committing every beloved feature to memory. Those beautiful lustrous dark eyes of his were hard and dark without even a redeeming hint of gold. Yet he still looked amazing, sleek and dark and devastatingly handsome. And even the thought made her feel guilty because she was lusting after her sister's husband, wasn't she?

Instead she opted to wonder what his precious lawyers had told him to do. Handle her with kid gloves? Give her no cause for complaint or any excuse to run to the press and tell all? Even after all they had shared, did he still think so little of her that he could believe that she would betray him like that? And what did it matter what he thought of her now when everything was over?

Topsy on her lap, she sat still long after he had departed. She had a new life to plan now, she told herself urgently. She didn't want to return to being a waitress. Living Brooke's life had made her more ambitious, just as the long struggle to recover from the accident and handle living with amnesia had made her stronger. She would look into other jobs and work out if she could qualify for a training course and take it from there. She might feel as if losing her sister for ever and then losing Lorenzo as well had left her with a giant black hole inside her chest, but she couldn't afford to give way to such feelings or they would eat her alive.

Right now, she was at rock bottom but, from here on in, her life could only improve...

CHAPTER NINE

THE NEXT MONTH passed painfully slowly for Milly.

She had no contact whatsoever from Lorenzo, but she received more than one visit from his lawyers, seeking affidavits and signatures to documents while also persuading her to consent to a DNA test. They kept her informed of her legal position and of what would happen next. And it being the law, it moved at a leisurely pace but, finally, the day of Brooke's funeral arrived.

The media storm that had erupted at the news of Brooke's death, and the half-sister who had mistakenly been identified as her, had died surprisingly swiftly, firstly because Brooke had become old news, and secondly because they could neither find Milly to ask her to tell her story nor identify the woman who was Brooke's half-sister.

Milly had lived very quietly, walking miles through the streets with Topsy to keep herself busy while struggling to suppress her memories of the time she had spent with Lorenzo. There was no point looking back to a relationship that should never have happened in the first place, she told herself sternly. He wasn't hers, never had been hers, and never would be hers again.

All the same, even in the midst of her grief there came a day when she could no longer close her eyes to the complication that had developed: she was pregnant with Lorenzo's baby. And a joy that laced her with guilt filled her almost to overflowing at a development that only *she* was likely to welcome. For too long, she had ignored her symptoms, and by the time she went to a doctor to have her pregnancy confirmed, she had already done a home test and had fully come to terms with the reality of her condition.

And that she had fallen pregnant really wasn't that surprising, she reasoned ruefully. She had had sex with Lorenzo countless times and no precautions had been taken. Lorenzo had believed she had an IUD fitted because at the time he had believed that she was Brooke and she hadn't had the knowledge to contradict him.

He would be upset when she told him, and Milly knew that eventually she would *have* to tell him. How could she not? He had a right to know his child—even if the woman carrying his child wasn't the one he would have chosen for the role.

Even when he had believed she was Brooke he had said, *'The last complication we need now is a child.'*

But she wasn't the same person she had been on the day of the crash, she recognised wryly. Her recuperation and dealing with life as an amnesiac in a rocky marriage had taught her that she was far more mentally and physically robust than she had ever dreamt. Neither of them were to blame for her pregnancy. She was happy about her child, even excited about her future. Lorenzo could hurt her, she conceded ruefully, but he wouldn't *break* her.

Those were the thoughts on her mind as she dressed for her sister's funeral, bundling her hair below a hat, doing her utmost to ensure that nobody would notice her and catch on to the powerful resemblance between her and Brooke. The lawyers had assured her that nobody expected her to attend. For nobody, she had read Lorenzo, and she had grimaced and had said that of course she would attend her sister's reburial.

A car picked her up at ten. The church was almost empty, there being few mourners this long after Brooke's demise but the paparazzi were out in force outside the church, peering suspiciously at everyone, in search of the half-sister they had heard about but had not yet contrived to identify. Her head bent, her slender body shrouded in a deliberately unfashionable black coat, Milly dropped into a pew at the back of the church, listening to the service while striving not to stare at the back of Lorenzo's arrogant dark head.

How could she think of him as the father of her baby when it wasn't even acceptable to approach him at the funeral, lest someone snatch a photo of them together? At the graveside, tears burning at the backs of her eyes for the sister who was gone and for the sibling affection she had never managed to ignite, she stole a fleeting glance at Lorenzo. He dealt her a faint nod of acknowledgement. His lean, strong face had a tougher, harder edge. He had lost weight. But then Milly had lost weight as well. She felt nauseous much of the day and it was an effort to remember to eat as one day drifted into another. Usually she tried to eat when she was feeding Topsy.

Lorenzo studied Milly from the other side of the cemetery. He hadn't wanted her to attend. He had needed her to stay in the background and out of sight, had assured himself over and over again that that was the only sensible solution. But there she stood, lost in the folds of a voluminous coat, her incredible hair hidden below a trilby hat, her delicate face shadowed by the brim and barely recognisable. She looked thinner, younger, but naturally she looked younger because she *was* years younger than Brooke had been. Milly would only be twenty-three on her next birthday he reminded himself doggedly. It was all over, *finally* over, the whole distasteful business of his marriage to Brooke, done and dusted, he reflected, fighting to block memories of his time in Italy with Milly: long golden days lazily drifting past, the scent and the taste of her, the sound of her laughter and the readiness of her smile.

It would do him no good to dwell on the past. He had married Brooke and it had been a disaster from start to finish. And Milly was Brooke's half-sister and by acting as her unofficial stand-in had knowingly engaged with Brooke in an unsavoury deception to fool innocent people. Evidently, she had seen nothing wrong with that kind of behaviour. In other words, the same thread of dishonesty that had run through his late wife like poison had an echo in Milly as well. But she could learn to do better with his guidance, he reasoned squarely. After all, nobody was perfect. And after the ordeal of living with Brooke, he wasn't perfect either because he found it very hard to trust a woman again. He had needed time away from Milly to recover from the fallout of his failed marriage and the drama of discovering that he had been living with another woman.

He remembered Milly cooking for him, remembered her giving him pleasure as he had never known, and his teeth gritted. It was done: the connection had to remain broken for the moment, lest the paparazzi go into a feeding frenzy over Milly's very existence. Hopefully, their interest in identifying her wouldn't last much longer. But were they to discover her and place her within his life, they would tear her apart, implying this, implying that, *hurting* her as she did not deserve to be hurt.

When the vicar had finished, Milly watched Lorenzo swing on his heel and walk away, wide strong shoulders straight as girders beneath his black cashmere overcoat, his back even straighter, and suddenly she couldn't bear it. In fact, her temper soared. So much remained unsaid between them and she didn't even have his phone number! What had she done that was so bad that he was treating her as though she didn't exist? And she *had* to tell him about the baby. She had no choice on that score. There was no way she was prepared to ring his lawyers and tell *them*! He owed her a hearing, didn't he?

'Lorenzo!' she exclaimed, darting frantically in his wake, her face heating with embarrassment at being forced to abandon her hard-won dignity.

Lorenzo wheeled to a sudden halt and turned back to face her.

'I need to see you to talk about something,' she told him in an angry rush. 'Do you think you could call round this evening?'

'Tomorrow evening. If I must,' Lorenzo gritted, his glorious dark golden eyes locked to her with an intensity that brought her out in goose bumps.

'You *must*,' Milly declared with bold emphasis. 'I wouldn't ask to see you if I didn't have a good reason for it.'

'Around eight, then,' Lorenzo confirmed coolly. 'Are you sure it isn't something my lawyers could handle?'

'No, it's too personal for that,' Milly retorted in a tight tone of annoyance, her colour higher than ever at being required to make that distinction.

'We'll talk over dinner. I'll pick you up at eight.'

Lorenzo strode towards his limousine, enraged at the shot of adrenalin now coursing through his veins and the undeniable sense of anticipation that powered it. He had been trying to stay away from her for weeks and she had just made that impossible, looking up at him with those haunting violet eyes. Of course, he could get through one dinner with her and behave! And go home *alone*? What was too personal? What the hell could she be referring to? Lorenzo did not like to meet anyone without knowing beforehand exactly what he would be dealing with. His strong jawline clenched hard.

He couldn't fault her behaviour, though, since she had moved out. She had asked for nothing from him and she hadn't gone to the press. She hadn't contacted him, hadn't clung, had, in short, done exactly as he had supposedly wanted. To all intents and purposes, they were finished. Only, it hadn't taken more than a day for Lorenzo to register that while he had acted in the shocked conviction that he didn't have a choice, absence wasn't what he wanted or needed from Milly.

He had told himself that he was free again, had wondered why he was so angry and why the knowledge that he was free wasn't the relief that he had expected it to be. And now he knew. Milly was looking skinny and that tore him up. Her fine-boned face was downright thin now and her ankles seemed too delicate to support her. In terms of weight there hadn't been much of her to begin with, he reasoned...but *was* she looking after herself properly? The idea that she might not be now that he was no longer around to watch over her welfare nagged at him and made him decide that a dinner was a very good idea because he could check her out without making a production out of it. And to hell with the paparazzi!

CHAPTER TEN

THE NEXT DAY Milly rushed round the apartment, feeding Topsy and tidying up. She hadn't slept well the night before, haunted as she had been by memories of her sister and the guilty strain of finally laying those memories to rest. Perhaps had she had more time with Brooke or more in common with her, they would have become closer.

Late afternoon, she took Topsy out for a walk and then let her out onto the roof terrace where she liked to wander among the potted plants. That done, she hurried into the bathroom and had a shower.

Why was she fussing about her appearance simply because Lorenzo would be taking her out to dinner? For goodness' sake, it wasn't a date! She would put on jeans and a sweater, she told herself, so that he could see that she had no silly expectations.

After the shower, she put on her smartest jeans and a simple top, but it was a heck of a struggle to get the zip done up on her jeans. Inexorably her shape was changing and, although she had got thinner, her breasts were still larger, her waist was expanding and her stomach was developing a definite outward curve. There was nothing she could do about any of that, she scolded herself as she examined her reflection and winced at the biting tightness of her jeans. She could tell that the need for maternity wear was only just round the corner.

Five minutes later, she tore off the jeans and the top and pulled out a dress instead, the pretty red dress she had bought when she was living with Lorenzo, only, unhappily for her, the dress was now much too tight over her boobs. In a feverish surge of activity she dragged out her entire wardrobe, trying on outfit after outfit until she found a sundress with a looser cut that was reasonably presentable even if it was a little odd to be wearing a sundress when winter was on the horizon. Lorenzo probably wouldn't even notice what she was wearing. He had hardly looked at her at the cemetery, after all, and once she told him about the baby, he would have much more important things to focus on.

At that point her nervous tension and worries threatened to overwhelm her. The discovery that she was pregnant had made a nonsense of her tentative plans for a better future in which she had planned to work while studying. There were so many things she wouldn't be able to do with a child dependent on her. She had hoped to move out of the apartment and sever her last ties to Lorenzo but how could she do that when she needed somewhere to live while she was pregnant?

The lawyers had assured her that, as William Jackson's younger daughter and Brooke's sibling, she was entitled to inherit Brooke's estate because Lorenzo had refused to accept it. But in her heart, Milly suspected that her half-sister would not have wanted *her* to benefit and that made her squirm. Brooke hadn't been fond enough of her and that made it even more difficult for Milly to contemplate being enriched by her sister's demise. She didn't feel entitled to Brooke's trust fund yet how could she refuse it when she had a baby on the way and desperately needed that security? As for taking any more money from Lorenzo, that was out of the question. Baby or not, she wasn't planning to hang on his sleeve for ever!

Lorenzo worked late at the bank and then headed straight to the apartment. That enervating word, 'personal', had played on his mind throughout the day. Did she still believe that she loved him? She had never mentioned love again after that first time when he had failed to reciprocate. Back then he had been relieved by that silence because he had still been planning to divorce her. After all, leopards didn't change their spots. He had never doubted that they would end up divorced and discovering that Brooke was, in fact, *Milly* had simply set him free sooner and more quickly than he had expected.

The dream scenario, his most senior lawyer had commented cheerfully, and Lorenzo had felt like punching him because the past month had been anything but a dream for him.

Milly opened the door with a fast-beating heart. Knowing that he was coming up in the lift had simply increased her nerves about what she was going to say. Lorenzo would be completely unprepared for her announcement and yet shouldn't he have become aware of the risk he had run with her the minute he had realised that she wasn't Brooke? Had that contraceptive oversight completely escaped his attention? She supposed it had, just as it had initially escaped her attention in the emotional turmoil of their break-up.

Lorenzo strolled through the door in a charcoal-grey pinstriped suit, blue-black stubble accentuating his wide mobile mouth and hard masculine jawline, imbuing his dark good looks with an even tougher edge. 'I can't work out what you could have to say that falls into the category of personal,' he admitted coolly.

'Believe me, it's very personal to both of us,' Milly retorted, annoyed by his continuing determination to keep her at a distance. 'I wouldn't have asked you here otherwise.'

Lorenzo gazed at her, dark eyes narrowed and shrewd, his attention lingering on the blue and white dress, which he remembered all too well. He remembered it best in a heap on the bedroom floor. He remembered taking it off to reveal her curvy little body. He remembered persuading her out of its concealing folds at a picnic and convincing her that they would not be seen in the shelter of the trees. Indeed, seeing her *wearing* it rather than seeing himself stripping it off her was a novelty, a novelty and a reminder that his libido didn't need. He clenched his teeth as a pulsing wave of arousal assailed his groin.

'Let's go to dinner and talk,' he urged thickly before he let himself down and just grabbed her and carried her back to his cave like a Neanderthal who hadn't seen a woman in years.

The soft blue cashmere stole she had put round her shoulders kept the chill of the evening air off her skin.

Lorenzo remembered buying that for her in Florence when he saw her shiver one evening. Indeed, he seemed to have an extraordinarily photographic memory for everything she had ever worn and everything he had taken off. The limo didn't have to travel very far before they arrived at a small bistro where they were immediately escorted to a dimly lit corner booth.

Lorenzo sank gracefully down. 'There's something I need to say first…'

'Go ahead,' she encouraged as she opened her menu.

'When you regained your memory, we needed a complete break from each other for a while,' he breathed tautly. 'You needed peace to come to terms with everything that had happened. I had to accept that Brooke was gone and deal with that appropriately. I couldn't have done that with you still living with me and I was keen to keep the press out of our relationship.'

'Yes,' Milly conceded uneasily. 'But, perhaps now you can accept that I have no desire to talk to the press *or* embarrass you in any way?'

'If you didn't crave publicity exposure, why did you agree to act as Brooke's stand-in and deceive people?' Lorenzo asked with unnerving suddenness, his disapproval of her behaviour obvious to her for the first time.

Milly flushed because she hadn't yet confronted the embarrassing fact that he viewed her actions as Brooke's stand-in as a form of deception. 'I didn't crave the publicity but it *was* exciting for me to wear her expensive outfits and to be greeted by people as if I was *somebody* for the first time in my life,' she admitted, mortified at having to make that lowering admission. 'But mainly I agreed to do it because I wanted to please her and help her out. It made me feel needed and I truly believed that it would make her fonder of me.'

Disconcerted by that honesty, Lorenzo frowned. 'Then you were very naïve. Brooke didn't like other women. She saw them as rivals and she didn't trust them. Did she pay you for your services?'

Milly reddened even more uneasily. 'She promised that she would but she never actually did. I was missing work and I couldn't afford to and still pay my rent. I once lost a job over it and had to move,' she confessed awkwardly. 'I didn't like to ask her for money and bring our relationship down to that level. I didn't want to be someone she paid like hired help. I wanted to be a sister coming to her aid and I hoped she would eventually appreciate that…'

As Milly fell silent to take note of the waiter hovering, Lorenzo frowned and voiced their selections while also ordering wine.

'How many times did you stand in for her?' he asked bluntly when they were alone again.

'The day of the accident would have been the fifth time but a couple of the times she used me it was simply a matter of me being seen entering or leaving a shop she was publicising,' Milly revealed, worrying anxiously at her lower lip with her teeth. 'But the last time? That was a big deal for me because I was to stay hidden in the hotel room she had booked for six days, which meant that I had to quit my job.'

'I've since learned where she was planning to go,' Lorenzo volunteered as the first course was delivered to the table. 'Brooke was flying to Argentina.'

'Argentina?' Milly gaped. 'Why Argentina?'

'Presumably to meet up with Scott Lansdale, because he was filming on location there,' Lorenzo supplied very drily.

'Scott Lansdale the *movie star*?' Milly

whispered in a feverish hiss, both incredulous and ironically impressed by that famous name. 'But he's a married man!'

'She was having an affair with him, probably in the belief that he would put her name forward for a part in his next film,' Lorenzo explained flatly. 'Brooke didn't sleep with men out of love or lust. She picked men she expected to advance her career. If they didn't deliver, she moved on.'

'You say that as if it happened more than once during your marriage,' Milly muttered with a frown, pushing away her glass when the wine arrived and opting instead for water.

'It did. Sex was only another weapon in her arsenal. After the first time I caught her out and she lied about it, I never slept with her again. We were living entirely separate lives by the time I started the divorce,' he completed.

'So, the rumours about other men weren't just gossipy stories like you first said they were?' she pressed in dismay.

'No, they weren't,' he confirmed steadily. 'At the time I didn't want to upset you by telling you the truth about our marriage... well, about my marriage with Brooke.'

Milly dropped her head, suddenly understanding so much more about Lorenzo. He had gone for a divorce as soon as he saw that his marriage was beyond saving. She could easily understand why he had initially steered clear of any further intimacy with her. 'Why on earth did Brooke marry you in the first place?' she pressed.

'Her trust fund didn't run to the designer clothes she adored and my wealth gave her unlimited spending power. Our marriage also propelled her up the social ladder, which gave her more opportunities to meet influential people in the film and television world.'

Milly swallowed hard. 'You think that she never loved you, that she just used you for what you could provide?'

Lorenzo shrugged and thrust his big shoulders back into a more relaxed position. As he shifted lithely his jacket fell back from his chest and the edges parted to display lean muscles rippling below the fine shirt and Milly's mouth ran dry as dust. 'She betrayed me so early in our marriage that she couldn't possibly have loved me. I never saw anything in her that made me think otherwise. I have to be truthful with you on that score. I didn't hate her, I certainly didn't wish her dead, but by the end of the first year when the marriage had died, I had few illusions about her character.'

As the main course was delivered, Milly breathed in slow and deep and thought of the way Lorenzo had looked after her after the accident, refusing to allow his own feelings to influence his attitude. That had taken an immense force of will and self-discipline that in retrospect shook her. But his strength and protectiveness had been powered purely by the mistaken conviction that she was his wife and deserving of his care.

'I'm glad that you felt that you could finally tell me the truth,' she confessed, wondering how the heck they had strayed so far from her intent to tell him that she was carrying his child. However, she didn't believe a public setting was suitable for such a revelation and resolved to tell him only when he had taken her home again.

'Hopefully that's cleared the air. Now, perhaps you'll tell me what was too *per-*

sonal to discuss with my lawyers,' Lorenzo murmured smoothly.

Her heart started beating very fast inside her chest, depriving her of breath, but she shook her head vehemently. 'I'll tell you as soon as I get home.'

His ebony brows pleated. 'Why the secrecy?'

'I don't want you to feel constrained by our surroundings,' she admitted stiffly.

When they stepped out of the restaurant, immediately flashbulbs burst all around them, blinding and startling her. As shouted questions were aimed at them like bullets by the paparazzi, Lorenzo curved a protective hand to her spine and urged her unhurriedly in the direction of the car.

'For goodness' sake, we shouldn't have come out together in public!' Milly gasped, stricken, in the back of the limousine. 'Why did you risk it? Before you know it, I'll have been identified.'

'And so what if you are?' Lorenzo incised impatiently between clenched teeth. 'Neither of us has done anything wrong and nobody knows what happened between us. It's nobody else's business either. But I do believe that it's past time for this relationship to come out of the closet and be seen.'

Taken aback by that far-reaching statement that suggested that they still *had* a relationship, Milly climbed breathlessly out of the limo and accompanied him into the lift. He leant back against the wall, all lean, sinuous male, his beautiful dark golden eyes intent on her, and desire clenched low in her pelvis, dismaying her because she had believed that she had better control than that.

'I'm not used to you keeping secrets from me,' he confessed. 'You were always very open.'

Milly recalled how she had told him that she loved him and barely restrained a wince at the recollection of how trustingly naïve she had been in those early days. 'I haven't changed but maybe I've learned a little more discretion,' she parried.

They emerged from the lift into the shadowy foyer of the apartment. Lorenzo strode ahead of her to hit the lights. Milly forged on into the lounge, leaving him to follow.

'So now...' Lorenzo drawled with wry amusement. 'I gather it's finally time for *the big reveal*.'

Milly breathed in so deep that she felt dizzy as she exhaled again and she braced her hands on the back of a sofa, reckoning that hint of amusement would be short-lived. 'I'm pregnant,' she informed him apprehensively.

Lorenzo did a complete double take, his dark head jerking up and back, his dark eyes gleaming sharp as rapier blades. *'Pregnant?'* he emphasised in astonishment.

Milly sighed as she sank wearily down on the sofa. 'I'm almost three months along because *I* wasn't using any birth control while we were together and *you* didn't take any precautions,' she reminded him.

Lorenzo hovered with an incredulous look stamped on his lean, strong face, his dark eyes glittering like polar stars. *'Pregnant?'* he repeated a second time as if he could not comprehend such a development. 'By...*me?*'

'Oh...are you infertile? You never mentioned it,' Milly shot back at him to punish him for that inexcusable second question, her colour warmer than ever.

Unexpectedly, Lorenzo dropped down fluidly into the seat opposite her, lustrous vibrant eyes fringed by black lashes pinned to her. Hurriedly she looked away, wishing he weren't quite so spectacularly handsome that he distracted her every time she looked at him. On some level her eyes were in love with those hard, chiselled features of his. But she needed to be cool, calm and collected, not tied in emotional and physical knots by her memories of her time with him, she reminded herself doggedly.

'I *could* be infertile,' Lorenzo mused almost conversationally. 'I don't know. Unprotected sex is a risk I've never taken with a woman…you're the single exception.' The instant he was forced to concede that point, he was plunged back into shock and the colour slowly leached from below his bronzed skin as her first words finally sank in. He stared at her, his dense black lashes framing his bemused gaze. *Pregnant?* How was that possible? But he now accepted that it was perfectly possible, even if he had not foreseen that possibility and that knowledge silenced him.

'But as you said, it's a risk you took many times with me,' Milly reminded him shakily, her courage beginning to flag because he still looked absolutely stunned. 'I'm not

Brooke. I didn't have the IUD you assumed I still had, and you didn't protect me.'

'No, I didn't,' Lorenzo acknowledged in a low, driven undertone. 'I just assumed it would be safe.'

'And I took your word for it.' Milly sighed.

'Madre di Dio,' Lorenzo groaned. 'I've always wanted a child but not like this.'

'I feel the same,' Milly admitted heavily. 'I've always wanted to be a mother, but this is hardly an ideal situation. Even so, I still plan to make the best of it. I won't be considering termination or adoption or any other way out of this situation. I *want* my baby.'

'I wouldn't have suggested those options,' Lorenzo asserted in stark reproof.

'Yet only minutes ago you were quite happy to suggest that this baby might not be yours,' Milly reminded him curtly. 'That was very offensive.'

'How am I to know who you might have been with in recent weeks?' Lorenzo countered in a driven undertone. 'The idea that you could be out there seeing other men has driven me crazy over the past month!'

Milly stared back at him in wonderment. 'I haven't *ever* been with anyone but you!'

she told him with a decided edge of bitterness. 'I was a virgin but *you* didn't notice… and although it hurt like hell I just thought it was a question of it having been too long since I'd last had sex, so I didn't say anything about it at the time.'

Lorenzo vaulted upright. 'You were a virgin?' he breathed rawly.

'Yes. And I was planning to stay that way until I was in a serious relationship,' she admitted with spirit.

Lorenzo raked long brown fingers through his ruffled blue-black hair. '*Dio mio*… I'm sorry. You should've told me that I'd hurt you.'

'I didn't want to spoil the moment…engaged as I foolishly was in trying to save my rocky marriage…the marriage that didn't actually exist,' she completed tightly.

'This…*us*…it is an unholy mess!' Lorenzo growled in sudden frustration.

'Well, I've told you now. Perhaps you would have preferred me to approach your lawyers with this little problem.'

'No. Not with anything that relates to our baby and, by the way, our baby is *not* and will never be a problem,' Lorenzo declared, moving restively about the room, obviously too shaken up by her news to settle again.

Our baby was a label that warmed Milly's heart and she hastily looked away from him, telling herself that she was simply relieved that he wasn't angry or resentful. He *wanted* their child. That was a more positive response than she had even dared to hope for. 'I'll make tea. I'm afraid I don't have any alcohol.'

Lorenzo flashed her a sudden unexpected smile that radiated charisma. 'May I have coffee instead?'

'Of course, you can,' Milly told him cheerfully as she jumped up, a sense of reprieve making her body feel shaky as she walked into the sleek kitchen.

'I want you to come home with me tonight,' Lorenzo announced with staggering abruptness from the doorway.

Wide-eyed with astonishment, Milly whirled round to face him where he lounged gracefully against the frame. 'Why the heck would I do that?'

'You're expecting my child,' Lorenzo countered evenly, as if her question was a surprising one. 'And you've lost a lot of weight. I don't want you living here alone.'

Her facial muscles locking tight with self-discipline, Milly turned away again to put the kettle on, grateful to have something to do with her hands. 'You threw me out, Lorenzo. I'm not coming back.'

'I didn't *throw* you out,' he argued vehemently.

'It's not worth fighting about,' Milly parried quickly. 'You were right when you said our relationship was an unholy mess. So, let's not dig ourselves into a deeper hole. Leave things as they are.'

'But I don't *like* how things are,' Lorenzo framed without apology. 'This child will be my child as well and I want him or her to have my full attention from the start. I can't achieve that if we're living apart.'

Milly's slight shoulders sagged wearily. 'I'm not sure I'd have told you if I'd known you were going to make this much fuss. I'm pregnant...deal with it,' she advised. 'And once you've thought us over, you'll appreciate that we were an accident that should never have happened. But that doesn't mean that we can't still respect each other and maintain a civil relationship for the sake of our child.'

Lorenzo's sculpted features had shadowed and set hard. 'I strongly disagree with everything you just said,' he responded in unambiguous challenge. 'I don't think we were an accident and nor is our baby. I want more than a *civil* relationship with the mother of my child. I'm a traditional man. I want my child's mother to be my wife.'

The mug in Milly's hand dropped from her nerveless fingers and smashed into a million pieces on the tiled floor. She jerked back a step to avoid being splashed by the hot liquid and then gasped as a tiny flying piece of china stung her leg, before stooping down in an automatic movement to pick up the broken china.

Lorenzo's hands closed over hers and yanked her upright again. 'Are you burned?'

'No,' she said limply.

'But your leg's bleeding,' Lorenzo pointed out, bending down to lift her unresisting body up and settle her down on the kitchen counter out of harm's way.

'It's only a little cut!' she protested.

Lorenzo yanked the first-aid box off

the wall and broke it open while frowning down at the blood trickling down her leg. Milly sucked in oxygen to steady herself, but she couldn't get her whirling thoughts under her control. All she could hear was Lorenzo saying, 'I want my child's mother to be my wife.' Had that been a marriage proposal? Surely not? That would be crazy. She blinked rapidly, wincing as he tugged the tiny sliver of china from her calf with tweezers and cleaned her up, covering the cut with a plaster as though she were a kid.

'Thanks,' she said as she watched him gathering up the broken china and cleaning up the mess she had made. Slowly, carefully, she slid back down to the floor and poured him a cup of coffee, extending it silently when he had finished.

'Yes, I *meant* what I said,' Lorenzo breathed in a raw undertone before she could speak again. 'I want us to get married as soon as possible.'

'You're not in a fit state to marry anyone, least of all me,' Milly told him roundly. 'A year and a half ago you were getting a divorce. Then your principles forced you into staying married and pretending. You got tangled up with me but that was only a sexual thing and clearly very casual when it all went wrong. Now you're single again. You need to start again with someone fresh. You've already walked away from me.'

'And look how that turned out for me!' Lorenzo urged impatiently. 'I'm back and I'm not leaving you again. And what we had *wasn't* casual and it *wasn't* just sex.'

'Maybe not on my side, *then*,' she specified with precision. 'But I was working blind in a marriage that was already dead, only I didn't know that. I assumed that I had married you because I loved you. Now I know that I was never married to you at all…and, Lorenzo, no offence intended, but I don't *want* to be married to a man who's only marrying me because I'm pregnant.'

'Well, at least I know you don't want me for my money,' Lorenzo replied with a wry smile. 'But you *know* that I want you and I want our child as well.'

'You can't buy me like a package deal. I won't come cheap or easy,' Milly responded, tilting her chin at him before walking back towards the lounge with her tea. 'Amazing sex isn't enough to base a marriage on.'

'Was I amazing?' Lorenzo probed huskily behind her and she almost dropped a second mug at the same time as an involuntary smile tilted her lips.

'You know you were…but then I don't have anyone to compare you to yet, so—' she protested jerkily.

'Yet?' he queried, removing the mug from her hand to press her down into a seat, setting the tea down on the coffee table in front of her. Glittering dark eyes pierced her. 'If I can't have you, no other man can.'

'I'm afraid it doesn't work like that.' Milly sighed. 'We are both free agents now.'

'You're not free while you've got my baby inside you,' Lorenzo shot at her, his lean bronzed face fierce and forbidding.

'When you've finished your coffee, you should leave. I'm sorry but I'm very tired. Between the exhaustion and the morning sickness, I tend to go to bed early most nights,' she confided. 'I'm not in the mood to argue with you—'

'I'm not trying to argue. I'm trying to make you see sense.'

'You're not getting any further with me than I got with you. You said you wanted to marry me, but I don't think you've thought it through,' Milly said anxiously. 'There's a lot more to marriage than sex and having a child together.'

'I know. I love you,' Lorenzo confessed without the smallest warning. 'I was going to wait another month before approaching you again. I suppose I was trying to be a better man than I am. I didn't want the newspapers writing stuff about you and upsetting you. I thought that if I waited long enough, they would lose interest in us both. But I can't *live* another month without you, so here I am being bloody selfish and weak!'

Milly heard only the first half of that speech and his claim that he loved her knocked her for six. 'You *can't* love me,' she told him weakly.

'I began to fall in love with you the day you awakened from the coma. I fell deeper in love with every visit. At first, I told myself it was just sexual attraction even though it had been years since I'd been physically attracted to Brooke. I assumed that once you recovered your memory you would switch back into being the Brooke I remembered, and I knew I would continue the divorce eventually.'

'But before we went to Italy, you said we'd see how things went for us.'

'By that stage, I was secretly hoping that you would *never* recover your memory and, to be frank, I really didn't have a proper game plan,' Lorenzo confided grimly. 'I only knew that I couldn't face letting you go. I had fallen head over heels in love with a woman who was kind and compassionate and loving and I was revelling in every moment of the experience.' A smile slashed his lean dark features. 'I was extremely happy with you and I want that back. But I want to do everything the right way round this time. I want you to be my wife.'

'Oh…' was all Milly could bleat at that moment.

'You're not saying a flat no any more?' Lorenzo was quick to recognise that she was weakening.

'I'm thinking it over,' Milly muttered, her cheeks colouring. 'Why didn't you at least phone me while we were apart?'

'I was trying to be strong for both of us and I thought we were safer from press intrusion if nobody, including you, knew how I felt about you,' he admitted grimly. 'But I found it very hard to cope without you. I buried myself in work. It didn't help. I came home at night and I couldn't sleep and the house didn't feel like home any longer without you in it.'

Milly began slowly to smile, and her hand crept up to frame one high cheekbone in a tender caress. 'I love you, Lorenzo. I've missed you so much.'

Lorenzo tugged her gently into his arms and held her close. 'How can you still love me after the mess I made of things?'

Milly jerked her head back playfully, a foam of silvery blonde ringlets falling against one cheekbone. 'If you were perfect, you'd be boring. But you must stop hiding stuff from me in the belief that I have to be protected from every adverse event. I'm more resilient than I look,' she told him firmly. 'Yes, there would've been unpleasant stuff in the tabloids if it got out that we were together but we could have got through it. We are stronger together than we are apart.'

His ebony brows pleated. 'I didn't think of that angle.'

'I know. Your glass is always half empty while mine is always half full,' she teased, her violet eyes sparkling as she gazed up at him. 'Let's not care what anyone says or thinks about us. I learned how to do that at school. You must've been more protected than I was. I was always the kid in the unfashionable shoes, who got free lunches because she was the poor foster kid...'

Lean brown hands framed her animated face. 'And now you're going to be the wife of a billionaire.'

Her nose wrinkled. 'It just goes to show... you *can* sleep your way to the top!' she joked.

'*Madre di Dio*... I love you so much, *cara mia*,' Lorenzo husked, his mouth crashing down on hers with all the hunger he had fought to suppress for weeks giving her the strongest message yet that he needed her.

They stood there kissing, urgently entwined, too long separated to bear the idea of being apart even for a moment, both of them studiously ignoring Topsy, who was barking at their feet. She backed him up against the window, wrenching at his tie

while he claimed urgent little biting kisses
from her luscious mouth.

'I gather I'm staying,' Lorenzo pro-
nounced with a wicked grin.

'Wait until you're invited,' Milly told him,
waited a heartbeat. 'You're invited.'

He carried her into the all-white bedroom
and dropped down on the side of the bed,
holding her between his spread masculine
thighs. He made a production out of sliding
down one strap on her shoulder and then the
other, pushing them gently down her arms
to her wrists so that the dress slid down bar-
ing the full swell of her breasts cupped in
a strapless bra. He undid the bra, let it drop
away, studying her ripe curves with rever-
ent intensity. 'You are perfect,' he breathed.

'You are not in the mood to be critical,'
Milly laughed, taking in his arousal clearly
outlined by the fine fabric of his trousers.

'Perfect,' Lorenzo repeated aggressively
as he splayed the gentle fingers of one large
hand across her stomach. 'You've got my
baby in there…and that means the world to
me.'

'And me,' she agreed as the dress fluttered

to her feet and he gathered her into his arms and settled her down on the bed.

For a long time afterwards, there was nothing but the sheer urgency of the passion they had feared they might never experience again together, and then, in the tranquil aftermath, the real world intruded again.

Lorenzo fanned her tumbled hair back from her face and stared down at her with an adoring glow in his intense scrutiny. 'We start again fresh from this moment with no ghosts from the past between us,' he murmured sibilantly. 'The house has already been cleared. I had mementoes put aside for you, photos and scrapbooks and such, but I donated the contents of the dressing room and the jewellery I bought her to a charity auction. It's all gone.'

Milly nodded uncertainly, surprised and relieved and sad all at the same time. 'We wouldn't have met but for Brooke,' she reminded him gently.

'I can't stand to think of a world in which I might not have met you,' Lorenzo confessed. 'So that is something to be grateful to her for.'

'If her trust fund does come to me, I'd

like to donate it to a good cause because I would never feel it was mine,' Milly admitted ruefully. 'I mean, our father never acknowledged me and neither did she really. She never once made me feel that she accepted me as an actual sister. It wouldn't be right for me to keep it.'

'As you wish. Just don't let the past poison anything that we share,' Lorenzo urged her anxiously.

Tender fingers stroked his roughened jawline. 'I love you too much, Lorenzo Tassini, to ever let that happen,' she whispered.

'I hope that means that you love me enough to get married soon,' he murmured softly, dropping a kiss down onto her reddened mouth.

Her eyes widened. 'How soon?'

'A couple of weeks?'

'No, that's far too soon,' she told him firmly.

'Well, if I had my choice it would be tomorrow,' Lorenzo admitted unrepentantly.

'Could we get married in Italy?' she asked wistfully. 'I'd love that.'

Lorenzo smiled. 'I think that could be arranged and still give you time to find a beautiful white dress.'

'I can't wear white. I'm pregnant!' Milly gasped with a wince.

'That's an old-fashioned concept,' Lorenzo overruled. 'You deserve to wear white and if I have anything to do with the decision, you will.'

Milly lifted her nose, knowing how bossy he was, resolved not to let him have anything to do with that decision. 'We'll see.'

'Is that you placating me?' Lorenzo asked suspiciously.

'Possibly.' Milly looked up at him, her whole face wreathed with happiness. 'I love you. I can't think of anything else right now.'

His dark eyes shimmered pure gold. 'Why should you think of anything else? I love you too, more than I ever thought I could love anyone, *bellezza mia.*'

Milly slipped into a dreamy sleep. Lorenzo lay awake planning the wedding and Topsy, suspecting that she wouldn't be welcomed into her usual spot in the bed, went for a nap underneath it.

Two months later, Milly adjusted her short veil and looked in the cheval mirror with a wide contented smile.

Her dress was a dream. Sheer lace encased her arms while a Bardot neckline exposed her shoulders and the fitted lace bodice drew attention away from the swell of her pregnant stomach, the tulle and organza layered skirt tumbling softly to the floor. Milly hadn't needed to hide her bump to feel presentable. She was proud to be carrying her little girl. It was only a few weeks since they had learned that they were to have a daughter and they both liked the name Liona. While Lorenzo was hopeful that Liona would inherit her mother's colouring, Milly was hopeful that she would inherit her father's.

Clutching her beautiful bouquet of wildflowers, she stepped into the car that would whisk her up the hill to the village church where they would take their vows. Lorenzo's senior lawyer had offered to lead her into the church and down the aisle. As they had become well acquainted during the proceedings that had established her sister's death and her own survival, she had laughed and agreed, especially after he had unbent sufficiently to admit that they had been taking bets in the office about how long it would take Lorenzo to admit that he had fallen madly in love.

Her eyes were intent only on Lorenzo when she entered the crowded church. A large number of Lorenzo's friends had chosen to accept their invitations and fly out for an autumn weekend in Tuscany. Many of them had already met her because once she had moved back in with Lorenzo he had begun entertaining again for the first time in several years. Initially her resemblance to Brooke had unsettled people, but once they had got talking to her and realised how friendly and unassuming she was that unease had melted away. In fact, for the first time ever, now settled and secure and confident in the happiness she had found, Milly was making friends.

Sunlight slanted through the stained-glass windows of the chapel, illuminating the man at the altar, who was very tall beside the small, rounded priest. His hair gleamed blue black in strong light, his eyes gilded to gold in his lean dark face and he was smiling at his bride and she grinned back, barely able now to dredge up the recollection of the forbidding, reserved and very serious man he had once appeared to be. He covered her hand with his. 'You look radiant,' he told her proudly.

And the ceremony began, short and sweet and with no flourishes, because neither of them needed anything fancier than the love they had for each other and the child that was on the way to make them into a family. A slender platinum ring was slid onto her finger and then one to his. Lorenzo kissed his bride without a second's hesitation, and they walked out into the sunlight smiling and united.

The reception was held in the village hall where the earlier civil ceremony had taken place. It was merry and fun-filled and utterly informal, very much in the bride's style. Lorenzo had bought a yacht, an uncharacteristic act of conspicuous consumption that had attracted a lot of flak from his colleagues, and in a day or two they planned to cruise the Caribbean for their honeymoon. That first night of their marriage, though, they returned to the peaceful farmhouse in the hills and ate by candlelight on the terrace with the stars twinkling above them before retiring for the night.

'Happy now?' she teased him as he helped unhook her from her dress.

Lorenzo spread the parted edges of the dress back and kissed a trail across her smooth pale shoulders. 'Yes, now you're officially mine. I feel safer being happy.'

'Nobody's going to take our happiness away from us,' she soothed, spinning round as the gown dipped dangerously low over her full breasts to fall to her waist as she slowly extracted her arms from the tight lace sleeves. 'We worked hard for it, and you earned it every week that you watched over me when I was in a coma.'

'I still don't deserve you,' Lorenzo breathed gruffly, trying without success to drag his attention from her truly magnificent cleavage.

Milly let the dress fall to her feet and stepped out of it. 'Yes, you do. You deserve your happy ending just like everyone else. And I'm going to be it.'

'No complaints here.' Lorenzo laughed, lifting her gently to set her down on the bed, stroking the firm mound of her stomach with a possessive hand. 'Are you tired?'

'More elated now that we've finally got here, where we wanted to be,' she confided quietly. 'It was a glorious day, exactly what I dreamt of.'

'I wanted it to be really special for you, *bellezza mia*,' Lorenzo confided.

'Believe me, it was,' Milly assured him, running her fingertips lazily through his luxuriant black hair, a shiver of sensual awareness quivering through her as his stubbled jaw rubbed across her nape. 'Oh, do *that* again,' she urged helplessly.

Her unashamed enthusiasm made Lorenzo laugh. 'I love you to pieces, Milly.'

'I love you too…'

'And that little girl you're giving us will be as special as you are,' he told her.

And Liona *was*, coming into the world with all her mother's zest for life.

Two years later, she was followed by Pietro, as dark in colouring as his sister was fair, and rather more serious in nature.

Four years beyond that, when their parents naively thought their family was complete, fate surprised them with Cara, blonde with dark eyes, a little elf of a child with a mischievous smile. And together they were the family that both Lorenzo and Milly had always dreamt of having.

* * * * *

Captivated by
The Innocent's Forgotten Wedding?
You won't be able to resist these
other stories
by Lynne Graham!

The Sheikh Crowns His Virgin
His Cinderella's One-Night Heir
The Greek's Surprise Christmas Bride
Indian Prince's Hidden Son

Available now